'It's such a relief that we got here in time,' Manolis said, taking her hand again in what seemed to have become a natural instinct. 'It could have been otherwise.'

In the moonlight she could see his eyes shining with happiness as he looked down at her. 'We could be such a good team you and I—I'm talking professionally, you understand,' he added quickly. 'It felt so right working together just now. We seemed to sense that…'

'Yes, I felt the rapport between us was… natural,' she said quietly.

He lowered his head and kissed her gently on the mouth.

Oh, those lips—those sexy, wonderful lips. She'd never thought she would ever feel them on hers again. She'd cried with frustration when she'd realised how much she wanted him, and he was never coming back.

But here he was.

Margaret Barker has enjoyed a variety of interesting careers. A State Registered Nurse and qualified teacher, she holds a degree in French and Linguistics, and is a Licentiate of the Royal Academy of Music. As a full-time writer, Margaret says, 'Writing is my most interesting career, because it fits perfectly into family life. Sadly, my husband died of cancer in 2006, but I still live in our idyllic sixteenth-century house near the East Anglian coast. Our grown-up children have flown the nest, but they often fly back again, bringing their own young families with them for wonderful weekend and holiday reunions.'

GREEK DOCTOR CLAIMS HIS BRIDE

BY
MARGARET BARKER

 MILLS & BOON®

First published in Great Britain 2009
Large Print edition 2010
Harlequin Mills & Boon Limited,
Eton House, 18-24 Paradise Road,   LP
Richmond, Surrey TW9 1SR

© Margaret Barker 2009

ISBN: 978 0 263 21100 9

Harlequin Mills & Boon policy is to use papers that are
natural, renewable and recyclable products and made
from wood grown in sustainable forests. The logging and
manufacturing process conform to the legal environmental
regulations of the country of origin.

Printed and bound in Great Britain
by CPI Antony Rowe, Chippenham, Wiltshire

GREEK DOCTOR CLAIMS HIS BRIDE

CHAPTER ONE

TANYA hurled the mop with the spider still clinging to it straight out of the window. It was a trick she'd learned from her grandmother when she had been very small and absolutely petrified of the giant spiders that had scurried along the floor of her bedroom.

"Just pick up a mop, dangle it over the spider and it will cling on, thinking it's found a friend," Grandmother Katerina had told her all those years ago, and it was still a good solution.

"Ouch!"

The sound of a deep masculine voice muttering a few choice Greek expletives rose up from the courtyard below her window. Tanya leaned out so that she could see the swarthy man beneath her and for a brief moment she thought she might be dreaming. It couldn't be…no, the low evening sunshine was playing tricks with her eyes…Manolis Stangos was in London, not here on the island…wasn't he?

"Tanya?"

"Manolis?"

"For a moment I thought you were Grandmother Katerina moving back into her old house."

He was speaking rapidly in Greek as if to a stranger, none of the smooth, silky tones he'd used when they had been together all those years ago. Tanya ran a hand over her long auburn hair. She was sure her afternoon cleaning session had done nothing to help her jet-lagged appearance. A cobweb was still clinging to her hand but thankfully the large scary spider was now scuttling away across the courtyard.

"Thanks very much! I know it's a long time since you saw me but I can't have aged all that much. Anyway…" Tanya swallowed hard as she rubbed a dusty hand over her moist eyes "…Grandmother—Katerina—died a few months ago…"

"I'm sorry. It's just that you were the last person I expected to see here."

His voice was softer now. Tanya took a deep

breath as she tried to remain calm. This unexpected encounter was playing havoc with her emotions.

"Considering it's now my house, I feel I've every right to be here."

"I'm getting a crick in my neck looking up at you. Aren't you going to come down and check if you've fractured my skull with that mop, Dr Tanya?"

He smiled, and she could see the flash of his strong white teeth in his dark, rugged face.

"News filtered through to me in London that you'd qualified. I always knew you would in spite of…in spite of everything that might have stopped you."

She looked down at Manolis and found herself relaxing.

"I'll come down and check you out, although you could surely do that yourself, Dr Manolis," she said as she turned away from the window, taking her time to negotiate the narrow wooden staircase.

By the time she'd reached the tiny, low-beamed kitchen, Manolis had come in through the open door. Nobody ever closed their doors on this idyllic island of Ceres where she'd been born. Doors were closed when you went out. That was to make sure a stray goat or donkey didn't wander in and help itself to the food in the larder, but the key to the house was always left in the lock on the outside so that friends and neighbours would be able to get in if they needed to.

Meeting up with Manolis again after six long years had almost taken her breath away. She'd forgotten how handsome he was. Eight years older than her, he must be…what? Quick mathematical moment…thirty-six, because she was twenty-eight.

She remembered them celebrating her twenty-second birthday together. She'd just told him she was pregnant. She remembered how shocked he'd looked, how confused she'd felt.

"OK, are you going to check whether you've cracked my skull?"

"Sit down, Manolis. You're too tall for me to check it when you're towering above me, and you make me nervous."

"Nervous?" Manolis laughed. "When were you ever nervous of me?"

He pulled a chair out from under the check-clothed table and sank down, spreading his long legs out in front of him. She remembered that as a child when the impossibly tall Manolis had come into her grandmother's tiny kitchen he'd seemed to fill the whole room. She'd tried so hard to get his attention in those far-off days but he'd barely seemed to notice her.

"Keep still, will you?"

Her fingers were actually trembling as she smoothed back the thick black hair that framed his dark, rugged face. How many times had she run her fingers through his hair? And yet her reaction had always been the same. That sexy frisson she got from simply touching him. It travelled all the way down through her body and before she knew it her legs were turning into jelly, and as for her insides—well, that was almost impossible to cope with at such close quarters.

She sat down quickly on a chair. Her eyes were almost level with his.

"I can't see anything wrong with your forehead. Not a mark on it. You're just making a fuss about nothing."

If she continued using her bantering tone she could cover up the fact that she was so deeply moved she wanted to give in to her impossible desire. She wanted to laugh and cry at the same time. She wished she could turn the clock back to the time when they'd been so deliriously happy, so madly in love.

Manolis stirred on the small hard chair, unable to believe that he was so close to Tanya again. He had to clench his hands to stop himself reaching out and pulling her into his arms. Desire was rising up inside him, that familiar stirring in his loins that wouldn't cease until they'd made love again. But that would never happen. He'd known when she'd turned down his proposal of marriage for the second time that he would never try again. She was lost to him for ever and they couldn't go back.

"I think you'll live," Tanya said as she resisted the temptation to place her lips on his forehead in the pretence that she was kissing it better.

For a moment she wondered how he would react if she gave in to temptation. She could try…but he had a hard look on his face now. The moment had passed.

"I've got to go," he said evenly.

"Does your mother still live on the end of the street? Are you visiting her?"

He hesitated. "She still lives there. But actually

I bought the house next to yours when I came back to Ceres a couple of years ago."

"Next door? In Villa Agapi?" She drew in her breath. Agapi was the Greek word for love. She had just come to live in Villa Irini, which meant peace. Love and peace next door to each other.

"Manolis, are you here on holiday?"

"I work here on the island again. I wanted to return and it was better for…"

He broke off as the sound of a child's voice came from the street.

"Papa, Papa? Where are you?"

Manolis hurried through the courtyard and stood by the open door that led to the street.

"Papa!" The little girl flung herself at him. He lifted her high into the air. She was laughing and screaming with delight as he lowered her into his arms.

Tanya remained absolutely still as she watched the joyous reunion of a little girl with her father. Her hands were clenching the side of the table to steady herself as she listened to the rapid non-stop Greek words that flowed from the child as she told her father she'd had the most exciting day. It emerged that she'd brought her papa a picture she'd painted at school but she'd put it down on a stone at the side of the path as she'd bent to take her shoes off because she hated wearing shoes when it was hot and the wind had blown it away and she wanted to paint another one now as soon as they got home because…

The story came out in one long breath. As she listened to the chatter, Tanya felt tears prickling behind her eyelids. This child, this beautiful little girl, couldn't be much younger than the child she'd lost. Their child. She and Manolis should have had a child like this one but…

"Chrysanthe, *agapi mou*," Manolis said, setting his excited daughter down on the cobbles of the courtyard. "Come inside and meet an old friend of mine. Tanya, this is Chrysanthe."

The little girl hurried across the small courtyard and through the open door of the kitchen, smiling, friendly, totally trusting.

Tanya tried to swallow the lump in her throat. This wasn't what she'd thought would happen today. It was all too poignant. Her confused emotions were draining her strength away. She reached out a hand towards the child.

Chrysanthe smiled as she placed her hand in

Tanya's. A pretty little dimple had appeared in the adorable child's cheek. Who did she get that from? Must have been from her mother. The unknown woman who'd obviously taken Tanya's place so soon after they'd split up. How could he have met up with someone and conceived a child so quickly?

"Do you live here, Tanya?" Such a lovely lilt to the lisping childish tone.

Tanya cleared her throat. "Yes. I've just moved in today."

"I like your hair." The little girl took her hand out of Tanya's and reached up to stroke her auburn hair. She looked up at her father. "Daddy, why couldn't my hair have been this colour?"

Oh, no, please don't say things like that!

Tanya heard Manolis's swift intake of breath.

"It's very…unusual," he said quickly. "You can't…er…choose which colour your hair will be when you're born. Sometimes the colour comes from your daddy and sometimes from your mummy."

"My mummy's got blonde hair but she says it's out of a bottle. Could I get some of this colour out of a bottle, Tanya?"

"You probably could, but I prefer your hair the colour it is."

"Like Daddy's?"

Tanya swallowed hard. "Yes, like Daddy's." Her eyes met Manolis's and she turned away to avoid the poignancy of this discussion.

"Did you have a good journey, Tanya?" Manolis said quickly, breaking the uncomfortable silence.

"I'm always relieved when I get here because it seems to take for ever."

"Where did you come from?" Chrysanthe asked.

"Australia."

"Australia? My daddy used to live there, didn't you, Daddy?" The little girl had started to speak English now. "He told me all about it. It's a long way from here, isn't it? It's got lots of croccy... What are they called, Daddy?"

"Crocodiles."

Tanya noticed his voice was husky. He was reaching down and hoisting his daughter onto his shoulder.

"Your English is very good, Chrysanthe."

"My mummy's English. Are you English or Greek, Tanya?" The little girl looked down at Tanya from Manolis's shoulders.

"I'm both—like you. English mummy, Greek daddy. But I was born here on Ceres."

"I was born in England but I like living here best. Daddy used to bring me out to stay with Grandma Anna and all my cousins. I love being in my grandma's house. It's such fun playing with my cousins. Look, I can touch the ceiling! Daddy, I can touch the ceiling!"

"Tanya, I'll take Chrysanthe away and we'll leave you in peace. I'm sure you've got lots to do still."

Peace! How did he ever think she could be at peace when there were so many questions to be answered? She'd come back here to escape her stressful life in Australia but had never imagined she would have to face the turmoil of the past. Yes, she'd come to find peace but that wouldn't happen now, not while she was living next door to Manolis.

Manolis cleared his throat. "I know you've had a long journey, Tanya, but would you consider coming out for supper with me this evening?"

She'd never heard him sound so nervous. As if he was expecting her to squash the idea as impossible. Well, she had turned him down just before they'd split, only to bitterly regret it when it had been too late to change things.

"That would be after I've settled Chrysanthe with Mother. She stays with her when I'm on call. My mother has a huge bedroom—with plenty of room for her grandchildren—and they all love to stay there. We're a very close family, as you know, and…"

His voice trailed away. He was looking down at her, his eyes betraying how much he wanted to see her again that evening.

"Yes, I'd like that. There are so many questions I want to ask."

"Me too. So, I'll call in about eight. We could go to Giorgio's."

"How is he?"

"His health isn't too good but he sits in the corner and watches the rest of his family do all the work." He turned away, one hand still holding onto the child on his shoulders. "Bend your head, my darling, as we go through the door."

"Goodbye Chrysanthe. Come again to see me." She meant it wholeheartedly.

"Ooh yes, I will. Daddy, I'm still taller than you. When I'm grown up I might really be taller than you. When you're an old man I'll put you on my shoulder and…"

The voices became indistinguishable as father and daughter made their way down the street. Chrysanthe was a beautiful little girl, but Tanya had never imagined that Manolis could have moved on so quickly after they had split up.

He'd moved on. She mustn't dwell on it. She would remember only the happy times. She found herself wishing that little Chrysanthe was her child but stopped herself as soon as the thought occurred. No regrets. She had to move on with her life and not spend time wishing for the impossible.

Upstairs again, she ran hot water into the half-size hip bath in her tiny bathroom. As a child she'd loved to be bathed by her Grandmother Katerina when she'd been staying with her. She'd never dreamed that her grandmother would leave this house to her. Katerina must have realised how much Tanya loved it.

Tanya stripped off and stepped into the warm water. Mmm, it was bliss to lie back with the bath foam she'd bought in the airport shop in Sydney only yesterday. It hadn't occurred to her that today she would be preparing to go out for supper with Manolis. Once more she had to remind herself that nothing had changed between them. And now that Manolis was a married man, the gap between them must remain wide.

She closed her eyes and smoothed some more foam over her skin as she leaned her head against the back of her bath…

Tanya woke with a start and her arms flapped around in the cold water as she heard someone calling her from downstairs. Above the bath she could see moonlight shining through the tiny little window.

Manolis stood downstairs with his hand resting on the wooden banister. "Tanya, are you OK up there?"

"Yes, yes, I'm fine." She hauled herself out of the bath, spilling water onto the tiles. "I must have fallen asleep."

Manolis heard the splashing water and had a sudden mental image of Tanya's slim, lithe figure emerging from the tiny bath where Grandmother Katerina had often bathed him when he had been a small child and his mother had been too busy to cope as she'd fed the latest baby. He was sorely tempted to ask if he could join her upstairs but he knew what the answer would be. Still, a man could dream, couldn't he?

He put on his sternest voice so that Tanya would have no idea how much she'd already affected him. "That's a dangerous thing to do— fall asleep in the bath. You should never do that!"

Tanya was already climbing the narrow wooden steps up to her bedroom, clutching the towel around her. If it slipped and Manolis looked up through the rungs of the wooden stairs that connected the kitchen with the top floor... She glanced down as she stepped off the stairs into her bedroom but couldn't see him below her.

"I know it's dangerous but the bath's so small my knees were up to my chin so it's unlikely I could have slipped under the water," she called breathlessly, as she searched for something to put on. Not the smelly travel clothes...how about these trousers? She pulled them out of her case along with new, lacy black knickers. They were to make her feel good, nothing to do with the fact that she was going out with the sexiest man on the island—in the world.

It took her barely five minutes to emerge from her room fully clothed in three-quarter cut-off denims, white T-shirt and flip-flops. She'd spent a lot of time swimming and running at the beach near the hospital just outside Sydney and rarely used make-up for a casual night out. She would blend in with the tourists in Giorgio's taverna. And she knew for a fact that Manolis preferred a natural-looking face—not that it was any concern of hers!

He turned as she came down the stairs and in spite of his resolutions he whistled. "Mmm, you scrub up well, Tanya!" he said in English.

She laughed. "You haven't lost the Australian accent you picked up, Doctor. Are you trying to make me feel at home?"

"Something like that." He moved to the bottom of the stairs, placing his hands, which seemed to have a mind of their own, on her shoulders. For a brief moment he hesitated before pulling her gently against him and kissing her on both cheeks.

"Welcome home," he said in the sexiest, most unplatonic tone. He hadn't meant to inject all that warmth and innuendo into his words but spending five minutes waiting for Tanya, knowing that she was first naked, then semi-naked then…well, it had played havoc with his intentions.

She tried to move backwards to escape his arms but she was pinned against the end of the banister.

She took a deep breath as she prepared to ask the big question. "Manolis, is your wife with you here on the island?"

"We're divorced. My ex-wife is in London," he said evenly.

She pushed her hands against his chest, making it quite clear that she wanted to escape this po-tentially dangerous embrace. There were too many questions that needed answers before she could begin to relax with him. But the fact that he was a free man made the situation a little easier…no, it didn't! Her emotions were already in turmoil.

"Let's go," she said quietly. "I'm looking forward to being back in Giorgio's."

She stepped out into the narrow cobbled street, terribly aware of Manolis's huge frame close behind her. She wasn't small by any means—her legs were long but she was quite short—so she'd always felt that Manolis towered above her.

Glancing up at him as they walked together over the uneven cobbles, she missed her footing. He put out a hand to prevent her falling as she stumbled.

"Careful!" He took hold of her hand. The touch of his fingers unnerved her completely. "This part of the street is so dark," Manolis said as he waved his other hand upwards towards the light at the bend in the street. "There! That's better."

White light flooded down over them. "I know every stone along this street. You'll soon get used to it. How long do you intend to stay, Tanya?"

She gave a nervous attempt at a laugh. "Good question. The shortest answer is I don't know. It all depends…"

"On what?"

"On how I feel after I've had some time here."

There was a comfortable silence before Manolis spoke again. "The only thing is, if you didn't have any plans to return to Australia in a hurry, I was going to put a proposition to you."

She took her hand out of his. No! He wouldn't propose to her again, would he? The clock could never be turned back.

As if reading her mind, Manolis said, "That was perhaps an unfortunate phrase to use. This is a professional proposition. You see, I'm medical director of the hospital here and we need another doctor because it's the beginning of the tourist season."

He paused and took a deep breath before continuing. "There is a hospital board of governors who have the final say when a doctor is appointed but I'm the one who assesses the medical credentials of a candidate."

She was still listening, even appearing slightly interested. Well, he could but ask. "Would you like me to put your name forward?"

Tanya remained silent as she reviewed all the implications. Manolis walked on beside her, making absolutely sure that he didn't touch her. He wanted to tell her that he would never propose marriage to her again. Two proposals, two rejections from the love of his life was more than any man could suffer. But they did need a good doctor at the island hospital and he did want to have her near him as much as possible while she was here. He had no plans beyond that.

CHAPTER TWO

THE emotional warmth given out by the revell-
ers, tourists and islanders in Giorgio's Taverna
welcomed and wrapped around Tanya as if she'd
never been away. As a small girl she'd been
carried in here many times by her parents, elder
brother, uncles, cousins and had often fallen
asleep on somebody's lap, the music lulling her
to sleep as the evening progressed. She would
wake up in her own bed either at home with her
parents or at Grandmother Katerina's, wondering how she'd been transported there.

Her brother Costas, who like his friend
Manolis was eight years older than she, would
sometimes tell her the fairies had carried her
home in a special coach that ran over the cobbles
without a sound. She'd liked to think that was
true and whenever she found herself falling
asleep at the table she'd made an effort to stay

awake so that she could enjoy the journey home. But, however she'd tried, sleep had always got the better of her.

Manolis was trying to guide her to a table, one hand gently in the small of her back, but many people wanted to talk to them as they passed by.

"Dr Manolis, come over here! There's room on my table."

"Thank you… I'll see you later on…" Manolis was smiling as he repeated his friendly phrase and moved on between the tables.

"I'm heading for that table in the corner," he whispered as he stooped down towards her.

Tanya was aware of the many glances in their direction. One middle-aged lady put out a hand to detain her.

"It can't be!" she said in Greek. "You're Katerina's granddaughter, aren't you? You're the absolute image of her when she was young and beautiful like you. Apart from the colour of your hair. You got that from your lovely mother, didn't you? I remember when she arrived here from England. Very soon she was going out with your father, our young Dr

Sotiris. Ah, he was such a handsome man."
She giggled. "All the girls fancied him.
Including me!"

The giggle turned into joyful laughter.

Tanya smiled, wanting to give the lady her full
attention even though Manolis was making his
impatience to move on very obvious

"How is your father? Still living in Australia?"

Tanya swallowed hard. "He died of cancer five
years ago."

"Oh, I'm sorry. How's your mother?"

"She's married again to an old friend. She's
happy."

She felt Manolis's hand putting pressure on
her to escape if she could.

"Lovely to see you again!" Tanya moved away,
still smiling as she and Manolis finally reached
the corner table.

Giorgio's son had seen them making their way
through the crowded taverna and was already
standing over the table they coveted, fending off
potential occupants.

"*Efharisto*. Thank you, Michaelis," Tanya said,
as she sank down on to the seat that was being
held out for her.

"Good to see you back, Tanya. Have you come to work with Dr Manolis in the hospital?"

She hesitated. "I'm not sure what I'm going to do. First I need some holiday and then... who knows?"

Manolis smiled. "I'm trying to get her interested in applying for the newly vacant position."

Michaelis shrugged his shoulders. "What is there to think about? Tanya, you would be ideal as an island doctor. We have a beautiful hospital now. Not like the old days when your father had to cope with a small surgery and not enough medical help. Come into the kitchen to decide what you want to eat. Mama has got everything laid out on top of the ovens. The chicken in mataxa brandy is very good!"

"Did your mother make it?" Tanya asked.

"Of course!"

"Then I'd love to have some."

"Me too!" Manolis said. "And bring us a small selection of meze to start with, *parakalor*."

The sound of Giorgio playing on his accordion drifted over the happy voices. In spite of the general clamour, as she looked across the table at Manolis she felt as if they were the only two people in the room. It was almost as if they were back in their favourite Greek restaurant on the outskirts of Sydney.

A bottle of wine was placed on their table. "On the house," Michaelis said. "It's from my father to welcome Tanya back to where she belongs."

Tanya looked across and mouthed her thanks to Giorgio. He raised a hand from his accordion.

"What a welcome!" Manolis said as he poured the wine. "Does it make you want to live here permanently?"

"As I told you, I have no plans at the moment," Tanya said. Her words came out more sharply than she'd intended.

Manolis reined in his enthusiasm. Tanya had always had a mind of her own. "I didn't intend to upset you," he said evenly.

"I'm not upset. I just need time to think. I came here for a holiday and I don't want to have to make any decisions while I'm still jet-lagged."

"Of course you don't. It was just an idea. Take all the time you need regarding the vacancy at the hospital. The post has already been advertised and we've had a couple of applications. The current doctor is returning to England to take up a post in London. He's not going until the end of the month but we're expecting an influx of tourists very soon."

Michaelis poured wine into Tanya's glass. Manolis put a hand over his. "I'm on call tonight, Michaelis, so would you bring me a bottle of still water?"

Michaelis called the order to a young waiter who threaded his way through the tables and poured a glass of water for Manolis.

Manolis was anxious to return to their discussion about the vacant position but he waited until they were alone before continuing.

"We particularly need someone who knows the islanders and someone like you who was born here is absolutely ideal. In the past we've had outsiders who didn't really understand what working on Ceres involved. So, at the last meeting of the hospital board it was decided that if we could find an islander with good medical qualifications, that would be the candidate we would take. As I say, you would, of course, be ideal but it has to be your decision. I know you have a mind of your own."

He gave her a wry smile as he said this. For a

few moments neither of them spoke. Tanya knew what he was referring to. She remembered that fateful day when she'd turned down his second proposal. How different her life would have been if she'd said yes.

She looked across the table. He lifted his glass towards her. "Here's to your stay here on the island, whatever you decide."

She raised her glass and took a sip. "I would have to be approved by the hospital board as well as you, wouldn't I?"

"Of course. We now do more operations than we used to. We're licensed to perform emergency operations when it would be counterproductive to try to get the patient over to Rhodes. And we do some elective surgery as well. So I'm still able to make use of the surgical skills and qualifications I needed in my previous London job as head of surgery. Our hospital grew from a very small surgery not so many years ago, as you will remember, so our rules here have to be more fluid than on Rhodes or on the Greek mainland."

He could feel his hopes rising as he saw the expression of increasing interest on her face. "But knowing the excellent grades you got in your finals and the fact that you're an islander born and bred, I know—"

"You know an awful lot about me." She looked across the table, her gaze unwavering. "Did you check my exam grades?"

He leaned back against his chair. "I contacted Costas around the time I knew you should have finished your finals. I wanted to make sure that…you were OK after…after everything that had happened. I knew you wouldn't have dropped out of medical school altogether but you might have needed to take some time off."

"I didn't take much time off."

"I think it would have been a good idea. Your health had suffered."

"Yes, yes." She looked around her. Nobody could hear what they were saying because of the noise. "You were probably right when you advised me to take a year off."

She swallowed hard as she remembered how confused she'd been after the miscarriage. She'd realised too late that her hormones and emotions had been all over the place. Still feeling that a baby was on the way and yet having to come to terms with the fact that she was no longer pregnant.

"I chose to continue and, of course, I didn't drop out of medical school. It had always been my dream to qualify as a doctor. All my life. Especially when I was very young and you and Costas were making fun of me or ignoring me completely. I thought to myself, One day I'll show you big boys and my dad I'm not just a silly little girl who enjoys playing with her dolls."

Manolis stared at her. He'd never heard her say anything like that before.

"I didn't know you felt like that." He paused and took a deep breath. "Were we awful to you, Costas and I, when you were growing up?"

Tanya attempted to shrug it off, wishing she hadn't been quite so vehement about something that had bugged her for years.

"Oh, you were OK," she said, lightly. "You were behaving like boys do when girls are around. Trying to be macho. Sometimes you even noticed me."

"We were only teasing you, Tanya," he said gently. "When you came out to Australia to begin your medical training I could see you were a force to be reckoned with. Ambitious, clever, full of potential. Wow, I wouldn't have dared to tease you then."

She smiled to try and lighten the mood she'd created. "Oh, you were wonderful with me— really supportive. I never felt patronised by the fact that you were a qualified doctor and I was only a student. It was just something I wanted to do for myself at that point in time. I suppose I was ambitious. I was one of the generation of girls who wanted everything. I didn't want to miss out on anything."

She lowered her voice. "When I found out I was pregnant I still wanted to continue with my studies. As I told you at the time, my mother had agreed to help me. You probably remember she was actually delighted at the prospect of her first grandchild."

Her voice cracked as she reached her final heart-rending words.

He leaned across the table and took hold of her hand. She remained very still but she could feel the prickly tears at the back of her eyes waiting to be released.

"I couldn't understand why you wouldn't

take time off," he said gently. "Why you wouldn't let me take care of you, why you turned me down when—"

"I think my hormones were jumping around too much. I wasn't sure if you were proposing because…well, because you thought it was the dutiful thing to do."

"Was that why you turned me down for the second time?"

"Manolis, let's defer this discussion, shall we?" she whispered. "I can see people looking at us."

"Of course."

She knew now she'd been mistaken to turn down his proposal. In the agonising weeks after they'd split up she'd realised how stupid she'd been. She'd destroyed the most essential part of her life. The love of the person she'd admired as a child and desired when she'd become an adult. And by the time she'd come to her senses it had been too late.

She swallowed hard, very aware of the big hand holding hers.

One of the young waiters put more meze on the table. Taramosalata this time to add to the kalimara and the Greek salad, all of which remained largely untouched.

Manolis held out a plate towards her. "Try some of these Ceres shrimps. You used to like them when your parents invited me for supper, I remember."

She removed her hand from his and took some of the tiny pink shrimps. "Delicious as always." She chewed slowly. "Some things never change."

"And some things do. You, for instance," he said gently.

She leaned back against her chair. "How have I changed?"

"Well…you always were stubborn but—"

"Stubborn? I suppose you mean when I didn't agree with something you wanted?"

He smiled. "Possibly."

She nodded. "I have to admit that some of the ideas I had when I was younger have changed. I don't think I would be quite so…well… stubborn, as you put it, now."

He wondered if he was in with a chance now with this older, wiser woman. No, of course not! If they were ever to become close again and he was to raise the question of marriage she would dash his hopes again. What did she mean when she'd questioned if his proposal had been merely dutiful? When the time was more convenient he'd quiz her further.

"So, you got all your information about me from Costas?"

"Mostly. We rather lost touch when he went to South America to work in that rural area. He hasn't answered any of my letters for ages!"

"He's chosen to live in a remote hospital near the Amazon. Sometimes he doesn't get his mail for weeks, months or at all. Often he can't get his letters sent out of the area. He's very dedicated to his work and doesn't have much spare time to worry about the outside world. My mother worries continually about him, of course, but she's adamant that he'll tire of this difficult life when he's had enough deprivation."

"He had a relationship in Australia that went wrong, I believe," Manolis said, quietly.

"Yes." She sighed. "These things happen."

Their eyes met and Tanya saw the moistness in Manolis's gaze before he looked down at his plate and began crumbling a piece of bread.

"You haven't drunk your wine."

Tanya took a small sip. "The jet-lag is getting to me. I'd better not drink it. It might make me sleepy and I want to stay awake. I feel that we…well, we're getting to know each other again."

"I was completely surprised when you turned up here today. I'd had no news of you for ages."

The people on the next table had now gone. He waited before he dared to broach the subject of their disastrous break-up again. He'd been so unhappy, so completely devastated and depressed that he couldn't imagine how Tanya had suffered when her physical health had been at an all-time low and she'd had to cope with the emotional confusion as well.

"I was so proud that you coped by yourself after I left Australia. It couldn't have been easy after…"

"After I'd lost the baby?" she said quietly.

"Yes. Costas said you went straight back to medical school."

"I was still in a state of shock, I think. As I said, I now know I should have taken some time off but I was very confused. Keeping busy kept me sane—or so I thought. You must have done something similar when you went off to England and almost immediately married."

She tried but failed miserably to disguise the bitterness in her tone of voice.

"Tanya! I…"

The young waiter was placing the main course

plates in front of them, having removed the scarcely touched meze dishes,

"Tanya, it wasn't like that!" he continued when they were alone again. "You'd made it clear that you didn't want me. My old tutor in London had already contacted me about a newly created post as head of surgery which he said would be perfect for me. I was holding off discussing it with you because I wouldn't have gone over to London without you. When you virtually sent me away I decided to go for it. There was nothing to keep me in Australia any more. Victoria and I were old friends and we just happened to meet up again."

"How convenient!" She couldn't hold back the jealous anguish she'd experienced when she'd heard that he'd gone straight into the arms of another woman.

She took a deep breath. "And then married and had a baby very shortly after."

"On the rebound, I suppose," he said quickly, regretting how much she must have been hurt when she'd found he had a child. "But in mitigation…I'm not trying to sound as if I'm in the dock being tried for something…"

She watched him, anguished about what he'd done but still unable to crush her feelings for him.

"Go on, Manolis, tell me why you're hoping to be forgiven for jumping from one bed to another in double-quick time."

His eyes flashed. "You'd turned me down, told me to go away, said I was making things worse for you by staying, didn't you?"

"Yes, I did," she said quietly.

"So, Victoria being an old friend helped to salve my wounds. Somehow the comfort she gave me turned to sex. She fell pregnant. We married in haste and repented at leisure, as the old saying goes. It didn't take us long to realise that we would drive each other mad if we stayed together. We split up when Chrysanthe was six months old. Victoria was busy with her career and agreed with me that Chrysanthe would be brought up well on Ceres with the extended family here. My mother was overjoyed to add another granddaughter to her brood, and I came over as often as I could. I was on a long-term contract at the time so I had to wait before I could give in my notice. When a vacancy came up here on Ceres I applied and was accepted."

"They must have been delighted to have you here."

He nodded. "Yes. After a while I was offered the newly created post of Medical Director. We've had to expand in recent years because of the long tourist season from April to November. Better boats, more tourist facilities..."

His voice trailed away. He hoped he'd helped to justify what had happened since he'd walked away from her. She'd asked him to go, but maybe, just maybe she hadn't meant it.

He gave a deep sigh. There he went again, giving himself hope that he could turn the clock back to the time when they'd been so idyllically happy together.

"Dr Manolis." The young waiter was standing beside his chair. "There's a lady in the kitchen who wants to speak to you. She's climbed all the way up the *kali strata* to find you. Her grand-daughter is having a baby in her house and there's some problem that I..."

The young man paused in embarrassment. Manolis was standing now, his hand on the young waiter's shoulders.

"I'll come and see her. In the kitchen, you say?"

Tanya was also on her feet. She'd heard what had been said and her medical training was taking over. She was holding her jet-lag in check as she followed Manolis up the three worn old stone steps that led from the main restaurant part of the taverna into the ancient kitchen with the moussandra platform in the high ceiling where Giorgio and his wife had first slept when the taverna had been their home before the six children had arrived.

The agitated elderly lady was sitting on a chair sipping a brandy that Giorgio had poured for her.

It took only a couple of minutes to elicit the medical information they needed. Manolis ascertained that there was someone with the woman who was in labour before telling the grandmother to stay where she was. Someone from the hospital would come to collect her later. Yes, he knew the house where she lived.

As they hurried down the *kali strata*, Manolis was on his mobile phone, speaking to the hospital maternity section, giving them instructions, telling them to send a midwife, a stretcher with a couple of porters, and have an ambulance standing by at the bottom of the *kali strata* in case an immediate transfer to hospital was required, as well as the medication and instruments he would require if that happened.

Tanya was trying desperately to keep up with him but the ancient cobblestones beneath her feet were treacherous and slippery and the moon was covered in clouds again. Manolis, sensing her difficulty, took hold of her hand.

"Nearly there," Tanya said in a breathless, thankful voice. "I know the house where this family lives. My father used to say the houses in this area are in the worst place to get to for an emergency. Neither up nor down."

"Exactly! And yet nobody around here has a phone," he said in exasperation as he reached for the old brass door knocker.

The door was opened almost immediately.

"Doctor! Thank goodness you are here. My daughter…"

Manolis and Tanya stepped straight into the living room where the patient was lying on a bed. A low moaning sound came from her as Manolis gently placed his hand on her abdomen.

"It's OK, Helene. I'm just going to see how your baby's doing."

Tanya had immediately recognised Helene as an old friend from her schooldays. Helene smiled through the pain as she recognised Tanya, holding out her hands towards her.

One of the hospital porters arrived shortly afterwards, carrying the Entonax machine that Manolis had ordered. He explained briefly that the maternity unit was very busy and they weren't able to send a midwife yet but that one would arrive as soon as she was free.

Manolis nodded. "That's OK. Tanya will assist me."

While he was examining the patient Tanya fixed up the machine and placed the mask over Helene's face.

"Breathe deeply into this mask, Helene," Tanya said in Greek. "That's going to help the pain. No, don't push at the moment, Manolis will tell you when. I know it's hard for you. You're being very brave."

Helene clung to Tanya's hand as if her life depended on it.

Manolis began whispering to Tanya in English. He was totally calm and in control of the situation but she recognised the urgency in his voice.

"The baby is in breech position. I'm going to have to deliver it as soon as possible because it's showing signs of distress and the heartbeat is getting fainter. Take care of Helene and don't let her push yet. I've tried to turn... No, it's too late, I'll have to deliver the baby now. Ask Helene to push now so I can get the baby's buttocks through... Yes, that's fine... No hold it for a moment—I'll need to do an episiotomy. Pass me that sterile pack." He took out a scalpel and some local anaesthetic injection and performed the procedure.

It seemed like an age as Tanya, almost holding her breath, kept her cool with the patient.

"Manolis has everything under control, Helene."

Please, God, she thought. Don't let her lose this baby. She knew the anguish of losing her own baby and wouldn't wish that on anybody. Helene had carried this baby to full term and she couldn't imagine anything worse than losing it at this late stage.

"The baby's buttocks are through, Tanya," Manolis said. "You can ask Helene to push. One last push should... There, brilliant!"

As he lifted the slippery baby up it gave a faint

mewling cry, rather like a kitten that had been disturbed from its warm, cosy sleep.

"Let me see, let me see my baby!" Helene held out her arms.

"In a moment, Helene," Tanya said, gently. "Manolis will—"

"Tanya, will you cut the cord while I put a couple of stitches in?" Manolis said quietly.

Tanya quickly scrubbed up. Taking the surgical scissors from the sterile pack, she cut the cord and wrapped the protesting infant in a clean dressing towel.

"You've got a little boy, Helene," she said gently as she put the baby in her arms. Tears sprang to her eyes as she saw the wonderful first meeting of mother and son. She dabbed her eyes with a tissue and held back the tears. She had to stay professional and think only of her patient. But she sensed that Manolis was looking at her. He was standing beside her now and had put a hand on her shoulder.

She looked up into his eyes and saw they were moist and knew he was thinking of their baby. She swallowed hard. How could she have hardened her heart and told him to leave her?

Why had he not understood in the first place what a miscarriage did to a woman? Would they ever recover from what might have been? Would it ever be possible to repair the damage they'd done to each other?

The future was impossible to predict. She would take one day at a time, but she knew without a shadow of a doubt that she wanted to stay here on Ceres for a long time, whatever happened. This was where she belonged.

She looked around the room, which had become rather crowded during the time that she and Manolis had been taking care of their patient. Standing near the door that led straight out on to the *kali strata* was a midwife, two porters and a young man who now identified himself as Lefteris, the baby's father. The midwife had held him back when he'd arrived a few moments ago.

"Baby's father is here, Manolis," Tanya said. "Is it OK if…?"

Too late! The young father had already sprung forward to embrace Helene and his son.

"We'll need to do some tests on your baby, Lefteris," Manolis said gently after a short while.

"He had a rough passage into the world and we need to check him over." He smiled. "Although from the way he's crying, there doesn't seem to be anything wrong with him."

The midwife came forward and said that someone from the postnatal team would do the tests as soon as they got baby and mother settled into the hospital. The ambulance was waiting at the bottom of the *kali strata* for them now.

As they emerged from the crowded room into the cooler night air Tanya took a deep breath.

"It's such a relief that we got here in time," Manolis said, taking her hand in what seemed to have become a natural instinct again. "It could have been otherwise."

His hand tightened on hers as he became animated about a subject close to his heart. "It's so strange here on the island. On the one hand we've got the latest technology at the hospital and on the other we've got people who haven't even got a phone living in a difficult place to reach, yet within minutes of help."

He broke off in frustration at the situation. "Sorry, Tanya. I don't want to offload my problems on you." He let go of her hand and turned her to face him.

In the moonlight she could see his eyes shining with happiness as he looked down at her. "We could be such a good team you and I—I'm talking professionally, you understand," he added quickly. "It felt so right working together just now. We seemed to sense that."

"Yes, I felt the rapport between us was… natural," she said quietly.

He lowered his head and kissed her gently on the mouth.

Oh, those lips, those sexy, wonderful lips. She'd never thought she would ever feel them on hers again. She'd cried with frustration when she'd realised how much she wanted him and he was never coming back. But here he was.

He raised his head and murmured against her lips. "So, do you want me to put your name forward as a candidate, Dr Tanya?"

Shivers were running down her spine. "Let's talk about it later," she murmured as she looked into his eyes.

She was making it patently obvious that she wanted him to kiss her again…

CHAPTER THREE

FROM somewhere in the distance Tanya could hear a cock crowing. She was hotter than usual. Where was she? She stirred in the strange bed and opened her eyes. Wooden rafters above her…where was the window?

The mists of her mind suddenly cleared. She was at Grandmother Katerina's, snug in the big bedroom at the top of the house. For several seconds she went back in time. She couldn't remember the end of the evening. She'd been in Giorgio's and… It was almost as if she'd been transported back here in the mythical fairy coach. There was a feeling of happiness tinged with sadness in the air.

And then she remembered. That kiss…that wonderful kiss! She'd murmured something to Manolis, held her face ready for another kiss, practically thrown herself at him. What did a woman have to do to make it obvious she would be putty in his hands? Oh, no! How humiliating to be rejected like that. Like what? She couldn't remember the details. Only the feeling that she'd expected Manolis to take her in his arms and...

She squirmed with embarrassment as she remembered how he'd made it clear that the kiss had been a one-off, the sort of thing that happened between old friends when they met again after a long time. Oh, he hadn't said that, in so many words. As far as she could remember, he hadn't said anything apart from suggesting they should get back.

At that point, the jet-lag she'd been holding off while she'd assisted at the birth of Helene's baby came back with a vengeance and she'd found herself agreeing with him. He'd held her hand but only in a courteous way so that she wouldn't slip on the treacherous cobblestones. As they'd reached Chorio, the upper town, they'd passed the door of Giorgio's Taverna where the door was closed but the revelry was continuing as always well into the night, and she'd found herself hoping Manolis would suggest they go in and join in the fun.

But they had kept on walking until he'd delivered her to her door and said goodnight. Not even a peck on the cheek! She told herself it was best they hadn't got emotionally involved. Too much too soon. Yes, Manolis had been very wise and she'd been stupid to think they could turn back the clock. There was too much between them to jump straight into any kind of relationship other than professional.

She began to doubt now whether she'd been too negative in her reaction to the idea of working at the Ceres hospital. She hoped that Manolis would put her name forward as soon as possible because, having worked with him last night and having had time to reflect on the proposition, she realised it would be ideal.

Her thoughts swung back to that idyllic period in her life when she and Manolis had lived together in Australia. The key stages of their relationship came flooding back to her. Their initial friendship when they'd first met again in the hospital, she a medical student, he a well-respected doctor. He'd asked her to have a coffee with him so she could tell him what she'd been doing since he'd last seen her on Ceres when she'd still been a schoolgirl of sixteen and he'd just qualified as a doctor at the grand old age of twenty-four.

She'd looked around her as they'd entered the staff common room she remembered. Seen the envious glances of the female staff as she was escorted in by this fabulously handsome, tall, athletic, long-limbed, highly desirable doctor. She and Manolis had seemed to be on the same wavelength right from the start of their new adult relationship. That evening he'd taken her out to a Greek restaurant near the hospital, wined and dined her, and she'd fallen hopelessly in love.

Four weeks later, at his suggestion, she left her hospital accommodation and moved into his apartment. It was pure heaven! Somehow she managed to keep her mind on her medical studies and clinical work during the day but, oh, the nights! In that amazingly luxurious bed that always looked as if a herd of elephants had trampled over it in the morning!

She never really worked out why the contraceptive pill she was taking at the time failed. Whatever had caused it, she was totally unprepared when she realised her period was late. She remembered the shock as the result of her preg-nancy test came out positive.

She experienced the awful conflicting emotions of wanting a baby with Manolis, yet wanting to plough on unencumbered to reach her goal of becoming a doctor as soon as possible. And then she realised that she could have both of these dreams. Many women had careers and children as well. She went to talk it over with her mother, who was truly delighted at the prospect of becoming a young grandmother.

She remembered the characteristic way her mother ran her hands through her still beautiful, shiny, long, auburn hair and pulled a wry face. "Not very good timing, Tanya, with your medical exams to get through, but don't you dare tell me you're not going to have my first grandchild! I'll take care of him or her while you're studying and working in the hospital. There won't be a problem…"

She saw the tears of happiness in her mother's eyes as she hugged her. When they separated her mother dabbed at her eyes with a tissue. "You go for it, my darling, and I'll be with you every step of the way."

"What will Daddy say?" Tanya asked tentatively.

"Oh, don't you worry about your father. I can handle him. He's a pussy cat really, although he may find it a bit irregular. Now, you run along and get back to that wonderful man of yours and tell him…well, break it gently. Men can be a bit strange at times like this but he'll come round to the idea if you give him time. I've known Manolis since he was a child and he's a good man. He'll stand by you. After all, it's not as if you got pregnant by yourself. It takes two to tango…"

When Manolis arrived back that evening she waited until after supper, having cooked one of his favourites, a chicken casserole. Then she told him the news. Oh, the shock on his face! She told him to sit down because he looked like he might faint. Then she joined him on the sofa. She told him she was definitely going to go through with it.

He said, "Of course you are!" Then he paused as if he was weighing his words. "And, of course, we must get married."

It was his tone of voice that had made her think he was simply doing the dutiful thing. He was still in a state of shock. She remembered her mother's words. *He's a good man. He'll stand by you.* Did she really want someone who was simply being dutiful?

"I don't think we should rush things," she told him.

"Are you saying you don't want to marry me?"

She took a deep breath before saying, "It's not as straightforward as that. I'm going to have a baby. Let's do one thing at a time. For the moment I want to make my preparations for being a good mother and also I need to get on with my studies."

But nothing prepared her for the agony of her miscarriage at fourteen weeks. It was all such a blur now. The sudden bleeding, Manolis driving her to hospital, being told she'd lost the baby, rushed into Theatre for a D and C.

She stifled the sob that rose at the back of her throat and looked out at the bright sunshine beyond the bedroom window, breathing deeply to calm herself again.

She had a sudden vision of Manolis standing by her hospital bed, telling her that he wanted to take care of her until she was well again. He was again asking her to marry him, to be his wife so that he could look after her. His voice had been so tender and kind. But she remembered the feeling of panic. Her hormones had been in control of her body, not she. She couldn't make decisions at a time like this when she was grieving for the baby that had died inside her. Couldn't commit to anything so life-changing as marriage.

So she'd looked up at Manolis and said she couldn't marry him. That it was best they separate until she didn't feel so confused. They'd only been together for a few months and everything had happened so quickly.

She turned her head to look around Grandma Katerina's bedroom, her bedroom now, and decided that was enough reminiscing for today. Time to get back to the present and continue with her new life.

No time for nostalgic reflection now! It was high time she got herself moving and sorted out her clothes. Just in case Manolis phoned to say she should go down to the hospital for an interview.

In the house next door Manolis stared up at the ceiling. He couldn't believe he'd passed up the opportunity of a night with Tanya. How often had he dreamed that she'd come back to him, that they were together again?

She had obviously been aroused by his kiss last night. Or had she just been pretending so as not to hurt his feelings? He could never be sure with Tanya. He'd lived with her for a few months, loved her, conceived a child with her and mourned with her when their unborn child had died in the womb. But he still couldn't understand her!

He remembered the night she'd told him she was pregnant. The shock of it had almost taken his breath away. He'd felt so guilty at giving her an added burden to the load of getting through her studies and exams. He had been so worried it would all be too much for her that it had only been in the next few weeks that he'd had time to begin anticipating how wonderful it would be to have a child with Tanya. She'd seemed so happy, and so capable of handling the situation that he'd begun to relax with her again.

She'd made it quite clear this was what she wanted, a child and a medical career. He'd realised that life was going to be wonderful when they were a family and not just a couple.

Then had come the awful evening when she'd

started to bleed. She had been fourteen weeks, he remembered. He'd driven her to hospital, made sure she was admitted immediately but there had been nothing anyone could do to save their baby.

He swallowed hard as the awful sadness of their loss hit him again. His grief had been almost impossible to bear. But he'd forced himself to stay strong for Tanya. He wanted to protect her, to take care of her while she'd been weak and vulnerable. That was when he'd made the mistake—he realised it now—of again asking to marry her. He'd told her that he wanted to look after her, to make sure as a doctor that she had the best treatment until she was strong again. He'd told her not to rush herself with her answer. He would wait until she was stronger.

But she'd looked at him as if he was a stranger. Her eyes had been blank, he remembered. This wasn't the girl he knew and loved. He'd worked in obstetrics and witnessed how hormonal a woman could be when she'd lost a child. But it would pass—surely Tania would realise that her current situation was temporary.

He looked up at the ceiling as he tried to bring

his emotions back under control. He hadn't been prepared for her rejection of him. She'd asked him to leave her.

He remembered going out through the ward door. Her mother had been coming towards him down the corridor. She'd put out her hand and taken hold of his. "It's best you leave Tanya alone for a while, Manolis. She's very confused. We're going to take her home for a while until she's strong again."

After she'd sent him away, rejecting the love he wanted to give her for the rest of his life, he'd felt he would never understand her. Not in a million years!

But last night, as he'd kissed her, he'd felt the desire rising in him as she'd snuggled against him and he'd felt that it might be possible to take this embrace to its obvious conclusion. But the old fears of rejection had nagged him. No, he'd been deluding himself, elated by the successful conclusion of a working partnership when they'd safely delivered Helene's baby together.

Oh, yes, she might have gone to bed with him. But he wanted more than a no-strings relationship with Tanya. But he could tell she valued her freedom. He could understand that now. She'd worked hard to become a qualified and now experienced doctor. She didn't need marriage.

Not like he did. As a young man he'd had two ambitions—one, to become a doctor and, two, to raise a family with the woman of his dreams. He'd had several no-strings relationships before he'd gone to Australia to take up a post in the hospital where Costas had been working. Meeting up with Costas's sister Tanya again when he'd been twenty-eight and she was a promising medical student of twenty-two had been like a bolt of lightning.

He'd been amazed when he had seen her for the first time for six years. The last time he'd seen her had been just before her father had taken the family out to Australia. He'd just spent his first year as a qualified doctor in the London hospital where he'd trained and had come over to Ceres for a short break. Tanya had been with Costas one time when they'd all walked down from Chorio to the harbour for drinks together as night fell.

He'd noticed she was growing into a very attractive young lady. But she had just been his friend's sister and far too young for him. But when he'd met her again six years later in Sydney he'd realised she was mind-blowing, with her fabulous, flowing, long auburn hair! Beautiful, attractive, intelligent, everything he'd ever dreamed of.

He remembered looking into her eyes, realising that she admired him too. Four weeks later he'd asked her to move into his apartment with him. They'd been idyllically happy until she'd told him she was pregnant. He'd been so worried about her, but he'd come to terms with it and relaxed, finally beginning to look forward to being a father. Then she had miscarried and their lives had changed completely. He had been totally rejected by the woman he adored at a time when he'd wanted to give her all his love and take care of her for ever.

The only way out of the impossible situation had been to start a new life and try to forget her.

"Papa!"

The sound of his daughter's voice brought him back to the present. She was downstairs, having come from his mother's house to see if he could take her to school. He always took her to school if he wasn't already working at the hospital. The school wasn't far away and the path was perfectly safe, but he liked to go with her.

"Chrysanthe, I'm coming, my love!"

The pile of clothes Tanya had brought from her suitcase to the bedroom could wait until she'd had some breakfast. She'd hardly eaten any supper at Giorgio's. She set off to walk round to the baker's to get some bread. As she stepped into the street, she caught a glimpse of Manolis turning the corner and the sound of his daughter's chatter. If she hurried she could catch him up before he reached the main street. No, she needed to cool down. She wasn't sure how she was going to face him today.

She lingered a while to make sure he was well on the way to Chrysanthe's school. She wasn't ready to face him just yet. Not until she'd made a cafetière of strong coffee and had some breakfast. He would probably phone later from the hospital and ask her down to discuss the job. At least, that was what she was hoping.

But he didn't! She spent the entire morning doing more cleaning, organising the kitchen, organising the bedroom, hanging up clothes, neatly placing her pants and bras in one drawer, her T-shirts in another, her swimwear in another…

"He should have phoned by now!"

She realised she'd spoken out loud. Maybe that was what happened to people who lived by themselves. She needed to get out more! The sun was shining outside. To hell with him! She wasn't waiting around any longer. She knew she really wanted this job now and so if he wasn't going to contact her she would go to the hospital and ask for it herself. Her father had been one of the founders of the new hospital, for heaven's sake! She would go in there with her head held high and ask to see the chairman of the board, whoever he might be these days.

Choosing the right clothes when you wanted to impress had always been a problem, because she preferred a casual look. Somewhere in the middle? Her cream linen suit? With a pale pink silk shirt underneath in case the heat got to her? Yes, that looked fine.

She sat down at her grandmother's dressing table. Looking in the mirror, she smiled at herself to remove the worry lines that had appeared on her forehead. At twenty-eight she needed to take care not to get real wrinkles settling there. The light tan she'd had since she'd gone to live in Australia needed very little makeup. A little foundation cream and a dash of lipstick was all she'd use. There!

Several strokes of the hairbrush smoothed out the long auburn hair and made it shine. She was glad she'd taken the time to wash it that morning. She could, of course, coil it up so that she looked more professional. Yes, that would definitely impress the chairman of the board, the old boy she was going to see. He was bound to be old, wasn't he? These types always were.

She piled her hair up on top and stuck it in place with several pins and grips. Over the years she'd practised this so often that it wasn't difficult for her. She immediately felt more efficient, intelligent, a better doctor, somebody that the chairman would take seriously.

"In short, Dr Tanya," she told her reflection, "you are the perfect candidate we've been looking for. The job is yours."

She smiled. "Thank you, sir. I accept."

* * *

Outside, the midday sun was stronger than she'd realised and the smart court shoes were hardly conducive to the cobblestones. Still, by the time she'd gone through the upper town and tried to persuade a taxi to collect her it would be quicker and easier to simply make her way on foot down the *kali strata*.

Halfway down, the door to Helene's house was wide open. Helene's grandmother was standing on the step and called out to her.

They chatted together. Tanya explained that she was on her way to the hospital and wouldn't come in for a drink. Yes, she would try to see Helene at the hospital and was glad that all was well with her. With praise ringing in her ears about the way that she and Manolis had delivered the baby, she continued on her way.

It was marginally cooler as she walked through the narrow streets of Yialos, the town by the harbour. The hospital, referred to by everybody as the New Hospital, was set back from the harbour near the church. It had started off as the doctors' surgery, she remembered, and had then been extended a great deal to qualify as a real hospital. It had certainly grown since she was last here.

She walked in through the front doors that led from the area where a couple of ambulances were parked. The reception area was very smart and, luxury of luxuries, it was air-conditioned! She really hadn't expected anything quite so grand here on Ceres. She began to feel slightly overwhelmed. And definitely overdressed. And the fact that she'd assumed she could just walk in and demand to see the chairman of the board was perhaps a little…

"Can I help you?" an English voice asked.

She moved forward to confront the white-uniformed receptionist who, unsmilingly, didn't seem as if she wanted to help at all.

"Actually, I was hoping to see…I'd like to make an appointment to see the chairman of the hospital board."

The young woman frowned. "Could you give me some details, Miss…?"

She cleared her throat and straightened her back. "I'm Dr Tanya Angelapoulos."

"Tanya!"

She turned at the sound of Manolis's voice—his most welcome voice! For a moment she felt like the young girl who'd craved his attention.

No, she was all grown up now and didn't need his help—did she?

He came towards her, looking so handsome in his theatre greens, a mask still dangling round his throat, that she was sure her heart missed a beat.

"I've been in Theatre all morning. I was going to call you when I got a moment to spare about the job. I haven't been able to contact any of the board. Wheels run slowly out here and now everything closes down for lunch. Why are you here?"

"I just happened to be down in the town, shopping, and I thought I'd drop in to…er get the feel of the place, see if I might like to work here," she improvised.

He looked taken aback, she thought, and wished fervently that she hadn't arrived unannounced. He didn't seem at all pleased to see her.

"Look, come along to my office. I'll fill you in on what's involved with the job." He turned to looked at the receptionist, who was desperately trying to find out what was going on. "It's OK, Melissa, I'll look after Dr Tanya."

He put a hand on her back as he guided her

out of Reception. He hadn't even noticed she was smiling.

Tanya could feel the gentle, soothing touch of Manolis's hand in the small of her back as they walked along the corridor. He was pushing open a door that led into a spacious room. He was obviously very important here. She'd noticed the sign on the door that read "HOSPITAL DIRECTOR." He was the one who'd got her interested in this job. Surely he could bypass the usual rules and sign her in?

As if reading her mind, he said, "If you've come about the job, I have to tell you we'll have to go by the book—at least in principle."

He waved an arm toward the seat at the other side of his desk. "There are only three men on the board, mainly chosen for their influence on the island. Two are retired doctors and worked with your father—so that's a definite plus. The other used to be mayor and can be a bit difficult."

"Manolis, I want to be appointed to this job on my own merit, not because the doctors on the board worked with my father."

"Of course you do, and you will be. You have

brilliant qualifications, hospital experience and background. I'll get on the phone as soon as everybody wakes up from lunch and siesta which, as you know, is obligatory on Ceres."

"I'd forgotten about the routine here on Ceres. I've been away for twelve years and the routines you follow here…"

She looked up into his dark brown eyes and saw them twinkle with amusement. "It's not so much routine as necessity, Tanya. After a long morning in Theatre I need a break. Some lunch—why don't you join me?"

He managed to make it sound like he'd only just thought of it, although he'd been wondering how he could drag it into the conversation without eliciting a negative response. Playing hard to get was more difficult than he'd thought it would be this morning. Trying to hold down his feelings for this woman was almost impossible.

She hesitated, just long enough to make him think she was considering her answer.

"Yes, I'd like that," she said, giving him a cool little smile, not too much, not too little. Hopefully, just cool enough to make him forget how she'd looked up into his eyes last night, practically begging him to kiss her again.

"OK. I'm going to have a quick shower. Help yourself to a magazine from the patients' waiting area over there. I'll be with you in a couple of minutes."

He was actually three minutes because she was timing him. She'd got a magazine open on her lap but the sound of the shower coming from his bathroom next door was tantalising her. She couldn't help thinking about that wonderful muscular body that had been hers all those years ago. Hers to snuggle next to in the night after they'd made wild, passionate love.

She remembered the way he would move languidly round to hold her in his arms again. And even though she'd thought she was exhausted she'd felt herself reviving, the whole of her body alive to his touch. She breathed deeply as she felt that even here. As she waited for him to finish his shower, she was becoming aroused. The thought that she could just walk across, open that door and—

"Hope you're not getting bored out here."

He stood at the other side of the room now, a

white towelling robe covering his magnificent body, one hand furiously rubbing his thick dark hair with a towel.

"No...you were very quick, really." She stood up, hoping she didn't sound too eager to agree with him.

He strode across the room.

How could he stand next to her dressed like that? She only had to reach out and take hold of that belt, give it a tweak and...hey, presto, they would be on the carpet in no time at all!

"Are you OK, Tanya?"

"I'm fine. Hungry, I think. Been a long morning."

She turned and deliberately moved into the patients' area to replace the magazine. She heard him close his bathroom door again. When he returned he was wearing hip-hugging jeans and a T-shirt. Now she really did feel overdressed!

They walked out through the deserted reception area. Everybody, it seemed, was on their lunch and siesta break.

"No doubt somebody is still in the hospital to take care of the patients and deal with any emergencies," she said as they moved down the busy street outside.

"Oh, we're all in touch by phone. And there are nurses in the wards, taking care of the patients. At the back of the hospital the accident and emergency unit is functioning as normal. But as much as possible we like to keep the work down in the afternoon."

They'd reached the harbour. Manolis slowed the pace as people milled around everywhere, tourists stopped in small groups chatting before deciding where to have lunch.

"Everything gets back to normal from five o'clock, doesn't it?" Tanya said. "I'd forgotten what life was like on Ceres."

"Yes, shops are closing now but they'll reopen when people begin to emerge for the evening. You'll soon be back in the swing of Ceres again."

He looked down at her and unable to contain himself any longer he reached for her hand. She looked up at him questioningly. For an instant she thought she'd glimpsed the old Manolis, the man she now suspected might have been totally committed to her. But she'd killed that commitment, hadn't she?

It would obviously be emotionally safer if she didn't try to resurrect what they'd had between them. Just get on with her life here on Ceres. Or should she tell him how, only weeks after she'd lost their baby she'd felt strong again and had come to her senses? Should she tell him that she'd regretted asking him to leave and missed him with an ache in her heart that was almost physical and wouldn't go away?

He'd dropped her hand again. She followed him to the table he'd selected outside Pachos Taverna. She remembered coming here with her family for evening drinks.

"Is Pachos still here, Manolis?"

"He retired a few years ago. His son has now taken over and he does delicious snacks at lunchtime. It's near enough to the hospital for me to pop out in the middle of the day if I'm not working. Would you like a glass of wine—or an ouzo perhaps?"

"A glass of retsina," she said, boldly. "Then I shall really feel I'm back on Ceres."

"I've got to work again this evening so I'd better stick to water."

A waiter came to take their order. They ordered Greek salad and Ceres shrimps.

"Nice and light, so that I can go out again for

supper," she said, hoping that didn't sound like she was angling for an invitation.

He hesitated. He'd been holding back long enough. "I'm working late tonight, otherwise I could have joined you." He hesitated, sure that she seemed disappointed. "I'm due for a day off at the end of the week. Would you like to come out in the boat with me?"

"You've got a boat?"

"Don't sound so surprised! I'm not as impoverished as I was when I was a junior doctor. It's my pride and joy, as you'll find if you come with me. How about Saturday? Are you free?"

She hesitated just long enough. Was she free? What a question!

"I think so."

"Well you can let me know. I'll be going anyway—and probably Chrysanthe. She loves the sea. We can—"

"Manolis!" A tall, distinguished-looking man was standing by their table. "So this is the mysterious young lady you've been keeping to yourself."

"Demetrius!" Manolis was standing, holding out his hand to shake the older man's. "I was going to phone you this morning but I've been tied up in Theatre. Dr Demetrius Capodistrias, let me introduce you to Dr Tanya Angelopoulos."

"Not Sotiris's daughter? Yes, of course you are. With that wonderful hair, you're the image of your mother."

Tanya felt a firm grasp as she extended her arm towards Demetrius.

"Do join us, Demetrius." Manolis was pulling up a chair. "Let me get you a drink."

"Thank you. What did you want to speak to me about, Manolis?"

"I was hoping you could convene a meeting of the hospital board fairly soon. Tanya is interested in applying for the post that's soon to be vacant."

"That's why I'm here. News travels fast on Ceres and when I heard that Sotiris's daughter had helped to deliver Helene's baby last night I knew I had to suggest she apply for the post. We need someone like you, born and bred on the island with a medical background." He smiled at her. "And rumour has it that your own qualifications are excellent."

"Actually, Manolis said there would be a vacancy for a doctor in the hospital soon so I've already given it some thought. I'd like to be considered if—"

"Splendid! I'll get in touch with the rest of the board this afternoon. Could you be free for an interview about six, Dr Angelapoulos?"

"Yes, of course."

"And you, Manolis. We'll need you there in your capacity as medical director."

"Yes, I'll be there."

Demetrius raised his glass towards Tanya. "I used to be a junior doctor when your father was in charge here. He was a great man to work with. We were all saddened, everybody who'd known your father, when we heard that he'd died."

"Yes." She swallowed hard. It still hurt.

"And your mother?"

"She's fine. Did you know she'd married again?"

"No, I hadn't heard that."

"An old friend of my father's. I'm glad my mother is content again."

Manolis's mobile was ringing. She could tell it was an emergency by the way he was speaking.

He stood up. "Sorry, I'll have to get back to the hospital. There's been a crash on the waterfront. One of the cars has gone into the sea and the passengers are being brought in."

"I'll come with you, Manolis."

Manolis hesitated. "I suppose it's OK for Tanya to help out before she's been appointed to the staff, isn't it, Demetrius?"

"In an emergency, we're relieved to get all the help we can. We have to be totally independent here on our small island. Our emergency rules have to be flexible." Demetrius turned to Tanya. "Thank you. I'll see you at six, Dr Angelopoulos."

She was glad to be busy in the hospital during the afternoon, with no time to worry about the interview in the evening. The first thing she did was to change out of the smart, inappropriate suit and put on a white short-sleeved coat.

The small accident and emergency unit was crowded with relatives and friends of the drivers and passengers of the two cars that had collided on the narrow waterfront road. The driver of the car that had gone into the water and the woman who'd been sitting in the passenger seat were being treated already by a couple of nurses.

Manolis immediately took over the treatment of the driver while Tanya tried to revive the unconscious woman whose lungs were waterlogged. Tanya turned her on her side and gently but firmly tried to remove the water from her lungs with an aspirator. Seconds went by before a loud gurgling sound indicated that the lungs were disgorging water. She started to cough and water now came up from her stomach.

She opened her eyes. "Where am I?"

"It's OK. You're in hospital." Relief flooded through her as she raised her patient to a sitting position and held a bowl under her mouth.

Meanwhile, she could see that Manolis had also been successful with his patient. The driver was already talking quietly, fretting about his wife, hoping everybody was going to survive. And how was the car?

Manolis gave his patient a wry smile. "Several metres under the sea, but everybody's alive, which is the main thing."

The two nurses took over from Manolis and Tanya, who were now required to deal with a patient whose leg was causing him a lot of pain. It wasn't difficult to diagnose that there was at least one fractured bone.

"We'd better have an X-ray of that leg. I'll do that because I know we haven't got a radiographer in the hospital this afternoon. Will you organise the plaster unit over there, Tanya?"

He put a hand on her arm. "Welcome to the real world of an island hospital! This is going to seem very different to the hospitals you've worked in."

"I know the score, Manolis. I used to watch my dad, remember. It was even more impromptu in his day."

By the time Manolis had X-rayed the distorted leg, he'd decided he would have to operate.

"It's worse than I thought," he told Tanya quietly. "I'll need to put in a steel plate and some screws in the tibia, which is shattered in several places. How much experience have you had in orthopaedic surgery?"

"I've assisted in Orthopaedic Theatre several times and passed my orthopaedics practical and theoretical examinations—with distinction," she added, just to set his mind at rest. "It won't be a problem."

"Excellent. The sooner we can get this leg in the right position again, the better will be the outcome for the patient. Check when the patient had his last food. I'll see you in Theatre when you've scrubbed up. The anaesthetist I've contacted should be with us shortly."

Minutes later she was standing across the other side of the operating table waiting for Manolis's instructions. The patient was anaesthetised and the anaesthetist was satisfied with his breathing. Tanya glanced at the monitor. Blood pressure was normal.

Above his mask Manolis's eyes registered calm. She'd never worked in Theatre with him before but she felt they were already a good team.

"Scalpel…"

CHAPTER FOUR

TANYA could feel the intense pressure under which the quickly assembled team was working. In this sort of emergency situation, where most of the team had expected to be off duty, the concentration required by them was paramount.

She watched as Manolis was cutting through the skin and outer layer of tissue to expose the tibia. As she'd seen on the X-ray, it was badly shattered. The front of the bone would require plating and other less damaged sections could be aligned with screws. In any case, whatever Manolis did, everything would depend on the healing process. If the bone didn't heal, amputation would be the only option.

As if reading her mind, Manolis began to explain to the team what he was doing and why. Whenever he was operating he tried to remember to pass on his skills to the team. He firmly believed that continual teaching was necessary in the operating Theatre. That was how he had learned. Textbooks were helpful but the real skills were learned by assisting and listening in the operating Theatre.

"We've got a young, otherwise healthy man here," Manolis concluded as he indicated to Tanya the steel plate he was going to insert. "There's no obvious reason why the bone shouldn't heal but always, in orthopaedic surgery, we cannot take anything for granted. Infection is always a possibility."

There was a murmur of assent from everyone. Manolis glanced across the table at Tanya. Beneath his mask she could tell he was smiling at her. The smile had reached his eyes. He was calm, totally in control, doing the job he was born to do—like she was.

For a brief instant she remembered the interview. She mustn't be too complacent about it. She wanted this job more than ever now she was actually working in the hospital. But now she had to concentrate on the work in hand. They had to save this young man's leg from amputation...

* * *

Three hours later, she pulled down her mask and breathed a sigh of relief. She was standing in the scrub room with Manolis, who was peeling off his gloves. A nurse and porter had just taken the patient to the orthopaedic ward. He was conscious now and Tanya had already removed his airway as his breathing was normal again.

"I'm quietly confident he's going to be OK," Manolis said, as he dropped the gloves in the nearest bin.

Tanya reached forward and released the Velcro fastening at the back of Manolis's gown. It was an automatic gesture which she'd done many times for whoever she'd been working with in Theatre.

Manolis swung round as he tossed the gown towards the large bin near the door. "It's a long time since you helped me to undress," he said, his voice much too husky and suggestive. He regretted the remark as soon as he'd made it. He waited for Tanya to retire into her shell again.

To his delight she smiled up at him. Her rich auburn glossy hair had tumbled down onto her shoulders as she'd removed the theatre cap that had been holding it in place. He remembered how it used to fan out on the pillow in the morning, all rumpled after a particularly fantastic night of sheer passion, love and...

"Purely second nature to me to assist the chief surgeon," she said, pleasantly but without a hint of sexual innuendo.

Good thing she couldn't read his thoughts! He reined in his feelings and physical arousal with great difficulty. They were standing so close now. Surely she could feel the emotional tension between them.

"I've got to go and see Helene in the postnatal unit," she said in the same tone. "I promised her grandmother I would."

He cleared his throat to remove all possibility that he would sound husky and provocative. "Don't be late for the interview."

"Of course not."

As she turned away she wondered how much longer she should put up the pretence that she wasn't interested in renewing their old relationship. They'd been standing so close just now. It had been all she could do not to take hold of his hand just to feel contact with him again. He'd had such a tense expression of control on his face.

As she walked out through the door she knew he was watching her. She could feel his eyes on her every movement. The door swung back again behind her and she walked away quickly before she had time to reveal her true feelings.

It wasn't going to be easy working with Manolis but she was determined to get this job. The old ambition was back. She still wanted to show him what she was made of!

She walked purposefully along the corridor towards the postnatal unit.

Helene was sitting in an armchair by her bed, feeding her tiny baby boy.

"Tanya! Grandmother said you were going to come in."

Helene patted her baby gently on the back as he finished feeding. A welcome burp came from the tiny mouth and she handed him to Tanya. "They checked him over but I'd like you to give your professional opinion."

Tanya ran her experienced eyes over the little body while she was changing his nappy to check that everything was in working order. As she removed his nappy a fountain of urine spurted into the air. They both laughed as Tanya narrowly missed being showered.

"He seems extremely healthy to me," Tanya said as she fixed a clean nappy and placed him back in his cot. "Have you got a name for him yet?"

"Lefteris, after his father."

They chatted together in Greek, both trying to fill in what had happened to them since they'd been together at school. Tanya was deliberately vague about her life in Australia, and managed not to mention that she'd had an affair with Manolis.

Helene began to tell Tanya about how difficult it now was that she and Lefteris were living with her grandmother. "It's kind of her to take us in but we're very cramped—it will be even more so now that our baby is here. You see, my parents don't approve of him. We're not married and un-married lovers don't live together on Ceres, as everybody knows. When I found out I was pregnant my parents were furious. It was OK for me to live at home, even at the ripe old age of twenty-eight, but scandalous to get pregnant. We had a big row and Lefteris and I moved in with Grandmother."

"Do you know why your parents don't approve of Lefteris?"

"They think he's a drifter, never had a proper job. He's worked on the boats for a low wage for years and now he earns very little as a casual builder and labourer. My parents have forbidden me to marry him. They say he'll leave me when he wants to move on again."

"Perhaps they'll change their minds now that your baby is here."

"I doubt it! We could go ahead and have a quiet wedding without spending too much money but I don't want to disobey my father."

Tanya put her hand over her friend's. "I'm afraid I've got to go now. I'm due for an interview with the hospital board at six o' clock and I need to change out of this white coat into something more presentable."

"Are you going to be working here permanently?"

"I hope so."

"So do I. You'll come and see me again, won't you? They're going to keep me in for a few days in view of the difficult living conditions at my grandmother's."

"I'll come and see you again as soon as I can."

* * *

The hospital board was assembled in a large office near the reception area. Manolis went into the room first and introduced Tanya to the three men, before taking his place behind one of the desks. As he'd explained to her, there were two doctors—Demetrius, who she'd already met, and another retired doctor. Alexander Logothetis, the ex-mayor who still had a great deal of influence on various committees, the island council, the school board and the hospital, was the third man.

Manolis had told her that Alexander Logothetis might be a tough nut to crack.

"We'll have to play down the influence your father had when he was doctor in charge of all medical services on the island." Manolis had told her just before they'd entered the room.

"Alexander is not much younger than your father and I believe they didn't always see eye to eye when Alexander was trying to climb the ladder of success in the property world here. There were several disputes between them before the new hospital project got off the ground."

She had looked up at him with confidence she didn't entirely feel. "Don't worry about me, Manolis. I intend to get this job on my own merits."

"I'm sure you will," he said, quickly.

The interview lasted almost an hour. By the end of it Tanya was feeling very tired. It had been a long day and she could feel the tension in the room getting to her. As Manolis had predicted, Alexander Logothetis was the most difficult member of the board to convince.

He'd asked questions about her qualifications, experience, health and stamina, hinting that it was a tough job for a young woman, with long hours and a flexible attitude required to every situation.

She'd answered all his questions at length and hoped she'd convinced him she would be totally committed to her work. The medical questions put to her by Manolis and the other two doctors were easier to handle. She had a wide range of medical and surgical experience and rarely had a problem with the questions that examiners put to her.

At last the board members started shuffling their papers around and Manolis stood up to signify the end of the interview.

"Thank you, Dr Angelopoulos," he said in a formal voice. "If you would like to go along to the waiting room, I'll call you back when the board has reached its decision."

He escorted her to the door and opened it. She stepped out into the corridor and he closed it without even looking at her. Oh, dear, was that a bad sign? Had she fluffed it? She walked along to the small waiting room. There was a drinking-water dispenser. She felt in need of something stronger to calm her nerves. How long would they be in there?

She sipped her water slowly.

In the interview room Alexander Logothetis was making his views abundantly clear. He pointed out that there were two candidates who'd been interviewed by the agency in London who hadn't yet travelled out to Ceres. They seemed keen to settle on the island.

"They're both straight out of medical school, without the experience of Dr Angelopoulos," Manolis pointed out succinctly. "Tanya's qualifications are at a higher level than theirs."

He'd already given a glowing account of her medical qualifications and experience, which had been of great interest to the two doctors but seemed to bore the ex-mayor. "Also, they haven't yet experienced life on this island. How do we know they will be able to improvise and adapt to difficult conditions as Tanya, having been born and bred here, knows extremely well?"

"Only yesterday Tanya helped Manolis to deliver a breech baby in a small house halfway up the *kali strata*," Demetrius put in. "That's when her ability to improvise was fully shown."

"I have heard about that incident," Alexander said icily. "And also it's come to my ears that this young lady doctor was actually assisting in an operation here this afternoon. Has anybody looked into the irregular insurance situation? You, as Medical Director of this hospital, Manolis, should have known better than to allow such a thing to—"

"When it's a question of a patient's welfare I will be the judge of whether to worry about insurance," Manolis countered vehemently. "In actual fact, I have already made provision with our insurers and ensured that a clause has been inserted in our policy for each emergency case to be taken on its own merits. Don't forget, Alexander, that you are the only non-member of the medical profession in this room. I will defend my right to improvise in situations of life and death without worrying about unimportant issues."

This time it was Alexander who remained silent. Manolis could see that he was seething with anger. He had to convince him that Tanya was the best candidate they were every likely to get on the island.

"Tanya went to see Helene and her baby here in hospital just now," Manolis continued evenly. "Helene and Tanya were friends at school. From what Tanya has told me, the baby is in excellent health and Helene is extremely grateful that Tanya helped to deliver her baby. As for the operation we performed this afternoon, without her help it would have been—"

"OK, Manolis," Alexander interrupted impatiently. "Let's take a vote on it. You've made it quite clear how you will vote. I shall vote that it would be better for us to see the two candidates who—"

"And meanwhile have Manolis run the hospital without the full complement of staff!" Demetrius interjected furiously. "And have to pay the expenses of the two young, inexperienced men who may prove just as unsuitable as the present outgoing doctor."

Demetrius banged his fist on the table. "He's resigned apparently because of what he calls the difficult working conditions on the island. Alexander, doesn't this prove the case for appointing someone who was born and bred here and totally understands these so-called difficult working conditions?"

Manolis knew this was the moment he had to play his trump card. "My secretary was making an important phone call when I had to leave her to attend this interview. She'd been notified earlier today that there was a possibility that the two other candidates may withdraw their applications. If we could hold off taking the vote a little longer until she's had time to—"

"It's time to take a formal vote, Manolis," Alexander said dismissively. "We shall know where we stand when everyone has voted."

A formal vote was taken. The outcome was a foregone conclusion. Manolis and the two retired doctors voted in favour of Tanya. Alexander Logothetis voted to postpone the appointment until all candidates had been seen.

There was a knock on the door. Manolis leapt to his feet. His secretary was standing on the threshhold with a piece of paper in her hand. "I've written out the details of the phone call, Dr Manolis."

"Thank you!" He glanced down and scanned the page before turning round, trying hard not to sound too triumphant. "Basically, gentlemen, it appears that both candidates have taken the jobs they'd previously applied for in London."

He paused for dramatic effect to give them time to let the news sink in. "Alexander, would you like me to re-advertise the post?" Another pause, still trying not to sound smug. "We could spend yet more hospital money on finding some other non-islander who is toying with the idea of working on a beautiful Greek island where they can spend their off duty sunning themselves on the beach…"

"OK, you've made your point, Manolis," Alexander conceded. "Under the circumstances I suppose—"

"The vote is carried in favour of Dr Tanya Angelothetis," Manolis declared, trying hard not to show how delighted he was, both on a professional and a personal level.

* * *

The sun was setting over the water down in the harbour as Manolis raised his glass of sparkling water towards Tanya. They'd both been busy after the interview, finalising plans for the work that Tanya would be expected to do.

Tanya sipped at her glass of wine, feeling excited about the outcome of the interview but apprehensive about the work she would be expected to do. She couldn't afford to let Manolis down when he'd been so supportive. She watched him now as he phoned his mother to find out if Chrysanthe was all right.

Even across the table, with the noise of the early evening chatter and laughter from the other tables outside the taverna, Tanya could hear the excited childish voice coming through on Manolis's mobile.

"Chrysanthe wants to speak to the pretty lady," he said, handing her the phone.

"When can I come to your house again, Tanya?"

She swallowed the lump in her throat. "You're welcome any time that Daddy says you can come. I've been very busy since I arrived but I'd love to see you again soon."

"*Daxi*. OK, Tanya! *Avrio?* Tomorrow?"

She looked across the table enquiringly at Manolis. He nodded. "Tomorrow's fine. I shan't expect you to work tomorrow after all the extra work you've done already. So…"

She waited for him to continue. He reached across the table and took hold of her hand. It seemed the most natural gesture to make but the touch of his fingers grasping hers was affecting her emotions deeply. Why was he looking at her in that whimsical manner?

"So if you happen to be at home after school, maybe Chrysanthe could drop in?"

Tanya smiled her assent as she continued chatting to Chrysanthe. "Did you hear that, Chysanthe? Daddy says it's OK if you come to see me after school."

The squeals of delight made her feel happier than she had in a long time. She looked across the table at Manolis, her heart too full for words as she handed back the mobile. It was almost as if the baby that they'd so wanted had materialised in this lovely child.

No, she mustn't fantasise! She must stay in the real world. This child wasn't hers—but this was what it would have been like if fate had allowed them to keep their baby, to move on and become parents.

Instead, Manolis had started another baby with someone else, just months after the trauma of losing their own, which was something she'd not been able to understand. How could he have resolved his emotional turmoil so quickly? It had taken her years—and it was still unresolved. She could never really trust him again—could she?

Oh, it was all so confusing…just like it had been when the miscarriage had happened. She should have got her emotions sorted out by now, shouldn't she? How long did it take to get over an ex-lover?

Deep down she knew she could never get over Manolis. He was the only man she'd ever really loved. Yes, she'd had other relationships. But nothing to compare with the intensity of emotion she'd felt for Manolis. He'd been her life, her love, her reason for living, the centre of her universe. She stifled a moan of anguish at what she'd demolished by asking Manolis to leave her by herself all those years ago.

She'd wanted to sort out her emotions, to

grieve for their baby by herself without any pressure about the future being put on her.

Some of the anguish she'd felt at that time was coming through to her again. She sighed as she realised she was going to have to work through this and decide if she dared give rein to her true feelings or…

"You're looking very solemn all of a sudden, Tanya." He frowned. "Are you having second thoughts?"

"About what?" she said sharply. It was almost as if he'd been able to see into her mind!

"About having Chrysanthe round to your house tomorrow? I'll try to get back early from the hospital to help you because I don't want to overload you with my family responsibilities."

"Oh, don't worry. It won't be a problem. Do get back early if you can. Obviously, it would be more fun the two of us looking after Chrysanthe. I'm sure she would enjoy having her dad and… me…at the same time…"

She leaned back against her chair, her eyes locking with his.

"You're a good father," she said quietly.

He hesitated. "I try to be." His husky voice trailed away.

They continued to look at each other, both instinctively knowing that the other was thinking about that other child which should have been theirs.

Manolis reached across the table and took her hand in his. "Are you thinking about...?" He couldn't finish his sentence.

She nodded. "Are you?"

He nodded, not trusting himself to speak.

Tanya leaned forward. "We need to talk about...what happened...when we split up."

Manolis squeezed her hand. "I think we should...if only to clear things up between us. Sort out where we go from here now that we're going to be working together."

"Exactly! So..."

He stood up. "I've got to get back to the hospital this evening. I'm doing a general practice surgery in a few minutes."

"I gathered you were going to be on duty when you ordered sparkling water."

He nodded. "But if you're going to stay down here by the harbour, I could meet you in a couple of hours for some supper."

"No, I've got to get back." Her words came out in a rush.

For a moment she'd panicked at the thought of the discussion about the past. She'd suddenly got cold feet. Was she really ready to face it head on with all the problems that needed to be resolved?

He was standing beside her now, looking down with an enigmatic expression, waiting for her to elaborate about why she had to get back, no doubt. She couldn't think of one reason why she couldn't enjoy a couple of hours here by the harbour so she remained silent. The thought of her empty house suddenly filled her with dread. But she really needed time to work out what it was she wanted.

To have him tell her he wanted to take care of her for the rest of her life? That she need never worry again if only she would play the little woman and let him do her worrying for her…as he had told her before? Well, not in so many words but that was how she'd worked out what he'd meant in her confused mind during and after her miscarriage.

Manolis looked down at her, his eyes troubled. He sensed she was going through some kind of emotional turmoil but he felt powerless to help. He'd been unable to reach out to her when they had both been trying to come to terms with the awful trauma of losing their baby. He hadn't understood what it was she'd wanted then and six years on he still didn't know! She must be the most complicated woman in the world!

"OK, I'll see you tomorrow, then, and we'll talk—yes?" He turned and strode off into the crowded harbour-side, back towards the hospital.

His hard, determined tone was ringing in her ears as she watched him until the crowd swallowed him up. The holidaymakers were still laughing and carefree but she felt a wedge of ice lodging on her heart. Once again she'd somehow managed to send Manolis away just when their troubled relationship was beginning to thaw out.

She made her way through the crowds towards the bottom of the *kali strata*, the steep cobbled climb that was the connection between Chorio, the older town at the top, and Yialos at the bottom. So many times she'd climbed this as a child, holding firmly to a grown-up's hand. She'd always belonged to somebody older and wiser than she.

But tonight she felt like a little lost girl with no hand to hold—and nobody waiting for her at home.

Reaching the top, she turned along her street and made her way over the cobbles to her house. From the end of the street she could hear the sound of laughter and chatter coming from the open door and windows of Anna's house. Manolis's mother was never alone. Always surrounded by her family, her children leaving their children in her care for a while or overnight.

She hadn't had time to go and visit Anna yet. She would make time tomorrow because she'd always loved her. As a child she'd always been welcomed into her house and treated like part of the family.

"Tanya!"

Chrysanthe's voice was, oh, so welcome at this moment of solitude as she was about to go into her empty house. She turned back into the street. The little girl was running over the cobbles, a beaming smile on her face, laughing for the sheer joy of living.

"Grandmother Anna wants to see you."

She had just time to glimpse the still good-looking older version of the Anna she remembered from her childhood before Chrysanthe grabbed her by the hand and began to tug her down the street.

"Grandma! I've found her."

Anna began walking up the street, her arms outspread. "Tanya! You haven't been to see me!"

"I've been busy, Anna."

The older lady hugged her. "I know, my child. Manolis told me about your job interview. How did it go?"

Tanya smiled. "Well, Alexander Logothetis was a bit difficult but—"

"Oh, that old goat! I hope you took no notice of him."

"I was polite but Manolis managed to convince him I was the right person for the job."

"I knew you'd get it! You clever girl. Passing all those medical exams. Manolis is so proud of you and so happy you are back here on Ceres."

Anna lowered her voice, even though Chrysanthe had already darted off into the house to rejoin her cousins. "I never did understand why you and Manolis split up in Australia. What was the problem? You were made for each other, you two! He came back home for a little while after you'd broken up. Devastated. Inconsolable!

But he wouldn't tell me what had happened. Me! His own mother! So…?"

Tanya could feel tears threatening to roll down her cheeks. "These things happen," she managed to say in a choking voice.

Anna, as if sensing she'd gone too far, put an arm round her waist.

"Come inside. You need a drink, my girl. Now, let me introduce you to some of my grandchildren. This little one is Rafaelo. He's Diana's first child. She's working in the pharmacy this evening. This is her baby son, Demetrius, and I was just going to feed him."

Anna picked up the feeding bottle from the bottle warmer.

"Let me do that Anna," Tanya said quickly. "You must be very busy with all these children around you."

Anna beamed. "My children are my life! What else would I do but look after my family? Here! Sit in this feeding chair. I've fed all of them on this chair—even Manolis. He was a handsome baby. I'll be in the kitchen, cooking, if you need me. You'll stay to supper, won't you? Keftedes tonight."

Anna smiled as she settled herself in the chair with baby Demetrius sucking contentedly on his bottle.

"Keftedes! How could I resist your home-made meat balls?"

She was totally absorbed into family life. Almost three hours had elapsed since they had all assembled around the large wooden kitchen table to eat supper. Baby Demetrius, who also needed some solid food, had sat on Tanya's lap while she'd spooned the semi-solid mixture of mashed potatoes and carrots into his mouth.

After supper Tanya had helped wash the children and put them down in their beds or cots. Chrysanthe had fallen asleep almost immediately.

"Will she sleep here tonight, Anna?" Tanya asked as she walked down the winding wooden staircase.

"I think it's better she does. Sometimes Manolis lifts her out of her bed and carries her back to her own bedroom, but tonight I'll suggest he leaves her."

"I must get back," Tanya said quickly.

"No hurry, child. Manolis will be home soon and you can— Well, talk of the devil!"

Tanya's heart skipped a beat as he appeared in the open doorway.

His face lit up.

"How was the surgery tonight?"

"Nothing too disturbing. I had to admit a patient with abdominal pains but I've checked him out thoroughly and the night staff are going to monitor his progress and call the doctor on duty if necessary. Which, fortunately, isn't me!"

"Well, I'll say goodnight."

"No, you won't!" He reached forward and put his hands on her shoulders, looking down meaningfully into her eyes.

"Chrysanthe is asleep," Anna said quickly. "I don't want you to disturb her. Leave her here till the morning, Manolis."

"In that case, Tanya, would you like to come back to my place for a nightcap?"

She looked up into those brown, melting, seductive eyes and all her resolutions disappeared.

How could she resist?

CHAPTER FIVE

MANOLIS closed the door behind them and for a brief instant he leaned against it, breathing heavily. He hadn't expected Tanya to agree to come back home with him. He hadn't expected her to now be looking up at him expectantly. If he took her in his arms now, would she vanish back into the dream he'd held onto for the past six years? He had to take that risk because he couldn't believe this was happening. But at the same time he had to consider her feelings. He knew how vulnerable she was. If he came on too strong, she would move away…

Oh, to hell with it! He was fed up with treading on eggshells around her! He reached forward and more roughly than he'd meant to he pulled her into his arms. To his excitement and utter amazement he heard her give a gentle moan. She was actually going to stay there in his arms while he…while he what? Dared he…dared he…?

He bent his head and pressed his lips against hers. She was so wonderfully pliant. He'd never thought she would ever mould herself against him as she was doing now…

Tanya moved to feel the maximum intimacy she could achieve without total abandonment. She had no idea why she'd thrown caution to the wind and she didn't care any more. She wanted so much to regain that wonderful relationship they'd had all those years ago. If only for a short time she would allow herself to pretend that they were both six years younger. She hadn't lost their baby, they hadn't had that awful row, she hadn't lost him, as she'd thought, for ever.

He was here with her now, his arms enfolding her, his body hard, muscles taut against her, needing her. Oh, she was so sure of how he needed her right at this moment! His manhood pressed hard and rigid against her own desperate body as his hands caressed her tenderly.

"Tanya?" he whispered as he held himself away from her for a brief moment.

She looked up into his eyes and saw that wonderful expression of total commitment that she'd once cherished so much, and had then destroyed.

She was aware that he was carrying her up the narrow wooden stairs. Once he bumped his head on the low ceiling of the ancient house. They both laughed and the tension relaxed. They'd been taking each other too seriously. Their previous relationship had been full of laughter, lightness, enjoyment.

She knew she could relax now. There was nothing serious about this romantic moment. They would make love...oh, yes, they would make love. Nothing mattered except this exquisite moment in time.

He put her down gently on the wide bed in the centre of the room. She was briefly aware of the moon shining through the window. A profusion of twinkling stars added to the mystery of the dark velvet sky. And then she saw it. A shooting star seemed to be coming to land in the bedroom before it disappeared without trace. She held her breath as she made the only wish possible.

"Tanya?"

He was leaning over her, his eyes full of concern. "Are you still with me? For a moment I thought I'd lost you."

"No, you hadn't lost me," she whispered. "There was a falling star and I was making a wish."

"What did you wish?"

"I couldn't possibly tell you or it might not come true." She reached forward to unbutton his shirt.

"One day perhaps?" He was gently removing her bra with one hand, the other straying inside to tease her rigid nipples.

"Who knows what the future holds?" She sighed as she anticipated how it would feel when their vibrantly excited bodies merged together…

She had no idea where she was when she awoke. Through the strange window a dark cloud was half obscuring the moon. The stars had vanished. But she'd made a wish some time ago…hadn't she? Or was that years ago? Now she remembered! She'd just repeated the wish she'd made a long time ago in Australia after they'd made wonderful, mind-blowing love…just like they'd done before she'd gone to sleep.

Manolis gave a soft moan in his sleep.

"Manolis?" She touched him on his shoulder, still hot and damp from their love-making. "Are you awake?"

He opened his eyes and smiled as he stretched his long muscular limbs like a tiger waiting to pounce.

"I am now," he murmured huskily as he wrapped his arms around her, holding her so close that it was immediately obvious why he'd moaned in his sleep.

As he thrust himself inside her she echoed his moan of pleasure. Why had she ever doubted him? Why had she denied herself of a lifetime of love that was too precious to have been destroyed?

They slept again after their love-making, this time with their arms around each other as if making sure that nothing could ever change between them again.

The sun was creeping over the windowsill when she awoke again. She stretched herself gently so as not to awaken him and also to make sure she still had arms and legs of her own! She seemed to have spent the night absorbed by this hunky, magnificent body which had taken over and melted inside her.

She lay back against the pillows, staring up at the ceiling, and suddenly reality hit her...and hit her hard. Where should they go from here? She had to be completely sure of her feelings this time around, now that she was older and wiser and had suffered the agony of separation from Manolis. She also had to be sure of how he felt about her. Oh, it had been wonderful to spend the night with him. But passion aside, she had to think clearly about the future.

Manolis was waking up slowly. He felt wonderfully happy but the old worries were crowding in on him again. Their love-making had been out of this world, just as he'd always remembered it had been. But now he had to tread carefully so as not to frighten this fragile girl away. He knew that in some way he'd been too demanding when they'd been in Australia. He'd possibly tried to take over her whole life. She was like a delicate butterfly who needed to be handled with care or she would fly away from him.

She'd been totally abandoned during the night, just like when they'd been together before their split. But now that it was the morning, would she have put up her guard again, decided she needed her independence and didn't want to commit herself to anything with him? He thought about it for all of two seconds.

One little kiss wouldn't frighten her, would it? He would test it out very gently.

Before the thought had barely formed in his mind he'd drawn her gently into his arms, his lips seeking hers. Oh, yes, they were still as soft and moist as he remembered during their love-making. Her lips parted as he kissed her.

He checked the temptation to make love again. Later, he promised himself as he raised himself on one elbow, looking down at her lovely face.

"We decided yesterday we needed to talk," he said gently. "About what happened to us the last time we were together. I think we both need answers."

She took a deep breath. It was now or never. "Yes, we do. Er…you first."

He swallowed hard. "Why did you send me away when I came to see you in hospital? I was so hurt by the way you treated me. You'd had a terrible ordeal, but I was also grieving for our baby. I couldn't understand why you were being so…" He broke off, unable to put into words the horror of his rejection.

"I'm sorry, I'm so sorry." She was trying to hold

back the tears as the memory of their last few moments together came flooding back to her.

He gathered her into his arms. "And I'm sorry if I was too pushy with my ideas for our future. When I asked you to marry me it was only because I wanted to take care of you."

"I know, I know…and I think that was one of the things I was scared of…losing my independence. We'd only been together for a short time. I was still very naïve. You were my first real lover—older and much more experienced than me. I'd never been on the Pill before and I managed to get unintentionally pregnant within the first few weeks of our relationship."

She gave a nervous laugh. "Then when I got used to the idea of having a baby I managed to make a mess of that. I was so confused by the speed at which my life had changed since I'd met you. And then you asked me to marry you. I realise now that my hormones were all over the place, adding to the confusion I felt about whether I wanted to commit to marriage."

"You make it sound like a life sentence."

"Well, that was how I saw it at the time." She softened her tone. "It was something I wanted eventually in my life, but there were so many things I had to do before I made an important commitment like marriage. But I didn't want to lose you. I wanted everything to revert to the way it had been between us." She paused. "And I never dreamt that you would go off and marry somebody else so quickly!"

"Tanya, I was devastated when you asked me to leave you alone. In effect you made it clear you didn't want any contact until you were ready to make it. I waited, heartbroken, for the girl I knew to come back to me and—"

"You didn't wait long. Six weeks after you left I went back to the hospital medical school to hear that you were working in London."

"Six weeks! You didn't want to know about me for six weeks!"

"You've no idea how ill I felt during that time! Then shortly after I started studying again I heard you were in a relationship with an ex-girlfriend. At that point I decided I had to try to forget you."

"Which was what I'd decided to do when you sent me away and didn't try to contact me. I saw no reason to stay in Australia when you didn't want me so I applied for and got the job in London."

"And who should you meet as soon as you arrived but your ex-girlfriend!"

She moved out of his arms so she could watch his expression.

He lay back on his pillow, looking up at the ceiling. "Victoria was actually on the interview panel."

"I don't believe it! How convenient! No wonder you got the job. No, I'm sorry. I shouldn't have said that. I'm sure you got it on your own merits. So what happened after the interview? Did you take her out for dinner, wine and dine her, like you did with me?"

She could feel jealousy rising up inside her. "How could you? So soon after…"

"You'd rejected me, told me stay away, you were better off without me! I was on the rebound. Victoria and I were friends and went out for dinner a lot. One night we both had too much to drink. We got a cab back to her place…"

"Fell into bed?"

"Something like that. First I'd drowned my sorrows in drink, then tried to forget you in the oblivion of another woman's arms. Classical situation for the rejected male. It was only when

I woke up the next morning the regrets crept in. Then we discovered she was pregnant and…"

Both of them were trying to ignore the shrilling of Manolis's phone. With a groan of frustration Manolis reached out towards the bedside table.

"I'd better answer it. It might be Chrysanthe."

"*Kali mera*, Papa!" squeaked a delighted voice at the other end. "Are you awake?"

For the second time, Manolis said, "I am now."

"Good. Because I'd like to come and have breakfast with you. Will that be OK?"

He ran a hand through his damp, rumpled hair as he tried to get his thoughts together. "You mean now?"

Chrysanthe was laughing now. "Well, of course now! What's the matter with you, Daddy? I'll have to have breakfast now or I'll be late for school. Grandma says she wants to give me breakfast with my cousins but I want to see you. I missed you last night because you didn't wake me up when you came home. Why didn't you wake me up?"

"I'm sorry, darling. We thought it best not to wake you. Grandma said you were very tired. Yes, come now for breakfast. Give me five minutes to take a shower."

Tanya was already out of bed, shrugging into her clothes. She would have a much-needed shower later but for the moment she wanted to make sure that she didn't shock Chrysanthe.

Manolis put out a playful hand to halt her from buttoning her shirt.

"Manolis, I have to go!"

His spirits sank as he withdrew his hand and went into the bathroom, deliberately closing the door so that he couldn't see how wonderful she looked half-dressed in the early morning light.

Five minutes later she was out of the door into the street, almost bumping into Chrysanthe who was eagerly skipping along over the cobbles to her door.

"Hi, Tanya. You're out early."

"Yes, I just came round to borrow something I need for my breakfast. Lovely to see you. I'll see you later this afternoon. Don't forget you're coming to my house after school."

"Oh, I won't forget. I'm looking forward to it."

"So am I."

She really meant it, but not right now! Not now when her body needed a good soak in the bath to remove the lingering odour of sex. As she hurried away she felt guilty at having spent the night with Manolis. This dear little innocent child. She didn't want to do anything that would upset her.

She closed the door behind her and made her way through the little courtyard into her kitchen and up the stairs as quickly as she could. Not until she'd peeled off her clothes and climbed into the bath did she begin to relax. She poured in some of her expensive bubble bath.

What a night! What a wonderful night! And she was glad they'd had their talk. At last they were beginning to understand each other again. So much had happened to both of them. It was essential they brought it out into the open. There had been far too much misunderstanding for far too long. She lay back amid the suds and simply wallowed in that wonderful post-coital, rapturous feeling that always came over her when she and Manolis had made love.

After a long soak and an effort to return to normality she'd continued sorting out the house, doing more cleaning and trying to get the place organised enough for her to entertain a five-year-old when she arrived after school.

The sound of a childish singing voice and the clattering of skipping feet outside in the street made her glance at the clock. Good heavens, was that the time?

"I'm here, Tanya!"

Breathless and excited, the little whirlwind was holding up her arms for a hug. Tanya bent down and lifted her up into her arms. She was warm and smelt of pencils and paint.

"Have you had a good day at school?"

Was that the sort of question children liked?

"It was OK. I've brought you a picture of my mummy. We had to paint one and take them home for our mummies to see but as my mummy's in London I thought I'd give it to you. Oops, it's got a bit crumpled. It'll look better when I've straightened it out…there! What do you think?"

Tanya put Chrysanthe gently on the worn rug that covered that part of the kitchen. Taking a deep breath, she held up the picture to the light coming in through the small window.

"Let's take it out on to the terrace, shall we? It looks beautiful to me. You're good at painting, Chrysanthe."

"My teacher said it was a good effort." Chrysanthe screwed up her face as she looked down again at her work, now a bit crumpled and grubby. "It was difficult to make it look like Mummy, you know."

"Is she very beautiful?"

"Oh, yes! I'm going to spend two weeks of my school holiday with her during the summer. She lives near a big park in London—I've forgotten the name of it but it has a lake in it and we go and feed the ducks."

"That must be lovely! Would you like a drink, Chrysanthe? Orange juice perhaps or…?"

"Orange juice, please."

Tanya went back into the kitchen while Chrysanthe settled herself on a chair by the small wrought-iron table in the middle of the terrace.

"You must be looking forward to going to see your mummy in London," Tanya said as she placed two glasses of orange juice on the table.

Chrysanthe smiled happily. "Yes, I love going over there. But I'll miss Daddy, of course—and Grandma, and all my cousins. But Daddy takes me there and brings me back and I love being on the boat and the plane with him and—Daddy!"

Tanya had only just noticed that Manolis had come through the kitchen and was standing on the edge of the terrace.

He smiled at the two of them as Chrysanthe leapt down from the table, knocking over her glass.

"Oops, sorry!"

"It's OK. I'll get a cloth."

Tanya pushed past Manolis as he lifted his daughter into his arms.

"May I have an orange juice?"

"Of course. Or something stronger?"

She was selecting a cleaning cloth for the dripping table and rinsing it before screwing it out. Manolis watched and thought she'd never looked so desirable to him. His heart ached for her to tell him that she wanted to start all over again.

"Something stronger?" she repeated. "I assume you're off duty for the day."

He gave her a wry smile. "Never assume anything when you're working at the island hospital. I'd better have an orange juice, please. I've got to go back in half an hour."

She handed him a glass of orange juice and put a fresh glass on the terrace table for Chrysanthe.

Chrysanthe was sitting on the floor, looking at one of the picture books that Tanya's grandmother had kept for her in the bookshelves by the kitchen door. Having discovered this treasure trove, the little girl was now oblivious to what the grown-ups were talking about.

Tanya sat down beside Manolis and took a sip of her orange juice. "I have to say the working hours seem very flexible at the hospital."

Manolis laughed. "You could say that. We have to cover any and every eventuality on the island. So one minute we're working as GPs in the outpatient surgery and the next we're scrubbing up for Theatre." He paused. "Talking of which— Theatre, that is—I'm operating this evening on Alexander Logothetis."

Her eyes widened. "Not our less than friendly ex-mayor? He seemed OK yesterday when he had all guns blazing at me during my interview. Did my appointment upset him too much?"

"He's had a suspected problem in the lower abdomen that could suggest appendicitis. A couple of times when he's been in pain I've taken him into hospital and given him a thorough examination, kept him in hospital for forty-eight hours, did all the tests that needed to be done. But after a couple of days or so the pain disappeared and I let him go home, calling him back into hospital every couple of months to be re-examined. He came to me last night when I was doing the GP surgery."

"Was that the patient you said you'd admitted?"

He nodded. "I kept him in overnight but I found his condition had worsened by this afternoon. He's now running a high temperature. I'm going to operate this evening."

Once more he paused. "I need another doctor with surgical experience. My surgical junior doctor has been on duty for nearly twenty-four hours. He's willing to assist me but really I need somebody who's not been working all day. Will you assist me, Tanya?"

"Of course! Oh, but what about Chrysanthe?"

The little girl looked up from her book at the sound of her name. "What about me, Daddy?"

She raised herself from the floor and pulled herself up onto Manolis's lap, still carrying the book. "Can you read this story to me?"

"I'm afraid I can't, darling. I've got to go back to the hospital."

"Do you need me right now, Manolis, or do I have time to read the story to Chrysanthe?"

He glanced at his watch. "I'll need you at the hospital to scrub up in half an hour. I'm leaving now."

"All right. Would you like to come here onto my lap, Chrysanthe? Daddy and I have to work tonight. If I read to you for ten minutes now, I'll finish the story tomorrow. Will that be OK with you?"

"Well, if you have to work at the hospital it'll have to be OK. Yes, thank you, Tanya." She snuggled closer to her nicely scented new friend. "I know that doctors have to work hard whenever they're needed. Daddy's told me that lots of times when he's gone back to the hospital. I'll go to Grandma's in ten minutes so let's get started, shall we? It's this story here, Tanya. Bye, Daddy."

"This was one of my favourites when I was a little girl. My grandma used to read it to me."

"Did you have a grandma in this house?"

"Yes, it was her house when I was small."

"What was her name?"

Manolis smiled to himself as he let himself out and began to sprint along the street. Ten minutes would pass too quickly for his little daughter, who had obviously formed a close bond already with Tanya. If only…! He daren't allow himself to think of what might have been if their own child had survived.

As he hurried down the *kali strata* he turned all his thoughts to the operation ahead of him. He hoped the anaesthetist he'd contacted had got himself back to the hospital. He hoped the results of all the tests he'd ordered would be back. He hoped the operation was going to be a success. It made no difference that this was a man who'd always been difficult with him. This was a patient who needed all the surgical expertise he could offer him.

Manolis stopped briefing Tanya as they scrubbed up side by side in the antetheatre. "I'm impressed you made it here in half an hour. Was it difficult to get away?"

"No, you've trained your daughter very well to accept the inevitable."

"She takes after her father," he observed dryly.

She decided to ignore that remark. "You were telling me about Alexander turning up at your clinic last night. What were his symptoms then?"

"High temperature, pain to the right of the groin around the appendix area. Just like on previous occasions. This time the pain was worse and the temperature was higher. I suggested we arrange to have him taken by our helicopter ambulance over to Rhodes to be under the care of a surgical consultant. He refused, saying that it would be just the same as last time. It would go away in a couple of days. So I admitted him here."

A nurse put her head round the door. "We're ready for you now, Doctor."

"I'm coming now. Tanya, final briefing."

"I've just checked the ultrasound and there appears to be an abnormality with the colon. I think we may find that the appendix is tucked behind the colon. Could be tricky to remove the appendix if it's stuck to the colon. That's why Alexander has been having recurrent pain and all these false alarms. I may have to take out some of the colon, depending on what we find when I open him up."

"Will you have to do a colostomy?"

"It may be necessary—I hope not. Alexander isn't the sort of man who would tolerate having to deal with a colostomy."

A nurse pushed open the swing doors that led

into Theatre. Tanya could feel all eyes on them as they took up their positions on either side of the patient.

She'd never felt so nervous in a hospital before! She looked across the table at Manolis and saw the crinkly lines around his eyes. And suddenly she felt totally calm, completely at peace with her chosen vocation. Her patient was safe with her. Manolis's hands were as steady as a rock. So were hers.

She cleared her throat. The Theatre was silent. No sounds except those made by the anaesthetic machine.

Manolis looked at the anaesthetist. "Everything OK with the patient, Nikolas?"

He nodded. "Yes, Manolis. Breathing excellent. Blood pressure slightly raised but not at a dangerous level. I'll let you know if a problem arises."

"Fine." Manolis turned back to look across the table again. "Then let's begin. Scalpel please…"

Three hours later they were finally able to relax. The patient was settled in a room with intensive care equipment right next to the night nurses' station.

Tanya leaned back against the cushion of the

wicker armchair on her terrace and looked across at Manolis, who was relaxing in the other armchair by her table, drinking the strong coffee she'd just made.

"I'm glad you agreed to hold our debriefing session back here," he said.

"Well, I decided if we stayed any longer in the hospital somebody would find something for us to do. At least this way we get to relax in comfort."

When Manolis had suggested they discuss the operation at his house she'd been adamant that it should be at hers. The memory of last night's love-making wouldn't help her concentration while they still needed to check out the details and make a report on the operation they'd performed that evening.

"I think we could say the operation was a success." Manolis was checking some notes he'd made earlier and adding to them. "I've given the night staff a detailed report already. I just want to make everything clear for all of us."

"It was a relief that we didn't need to do a colostomy. You took a large section of colon, didn't you?"

"I had to in order to get at the appendix, which

was tucked behind it as I thought, and I didn't want to try to separate the organs in case there was some malignancy there. If there's a trace of cancer it could spread to other areas of the body. You did put those biopsies into the path lab for checking tonight, didn't you?"

She nodded. "Of course. The pathologist on call was none too pleased when I phoned him, but he's agreed to come in and get on with the tests."

"Good. The sooner we can rule out malignancy, the sooner Alexander will be happy. And he can be an impatient man, as we both know."

"And irascible, cantankerous, difficult…"

He laughed. "Can't think why we saved the old—"

"Manolis! How can you say such a thing?"

"Only joking! A patient is a patient and they all get the same excellent treatment whatever we think about them. Will you go in and see him first thing in the morning, Tanya?"

"How first thing? It's nearly midnight now."

"Oh, eight o' clock, if you can make it. I'll be in by half past. I need to take Chrysanthe to school. Her teacher wants to see me about something." He paused. "Now, that's the end of our working day so no more talking shop. And I've made sure that we don't get called out again tonight by designating one of the surgical team to stay on the premises and be on hand for any eventuality. And I've got absolute faith in our excellent night sister."

He picked up both coffee cups and went into the kitchen. "I'll go and get a bottle of wine from my fridge."

Manolis disappeared next door. She felt totally exhausted but when he reappeared she came to life again.

"Where do you keep your corkscrew?"

"I don't know. In the knife drawer by the sink, I suppose, although I doubt if Grandma drank wine at home."

She joined him in the kitchen and found him already searching where she'd suggested.

"I'll have to get the kitchen sorted out. Oh, look, here it is—in with the clean dusters. Funny place to put it."

She turned round triumphantly, holding it in her hands. "Da-dah!"

He'd been right behind her, leaning over her, in fact. They were so close again.

He reached for the corkscrew and put it down on the draining board while with his other hand he drew her even closer, lowering his head to kiss her, gently at first but when he felt her responding he became daring again. Memories of their previous night of passion were bringing him hope that their relationship might be moving on. It hadn't been just a one-off for old times' sake.

A sigh escaped her lips as he released her from his arms and looked down at her quizzically, trying to gauge her mood. Deftly, he began to unbutton her shirt, his fingers unsure of how quickly to move, however, as he willed her to feel some of the excitement that being close together always generated.

His tantalising fingers were on her breasts, gently coaxing her into a state of impossible arousal. She could feel herself melting as her desire rose. Her heart was winning the contest. She was going with the flow, entering that well-remembered paradise in which there was no yesterday, no tomorrow, just the present…

She could tell she was in her own bed as she came round from a deep sleep. Her limbs felt delightfully relaxed. In fact, her whole body had a fluid feeling, as if she'd been swimming in a warm tropical pool all night.

She turned her head. In the early morning light coming through the tiny window beside the bed she could see the outline of Manolis's features. Oh, he looked so wonderfully desirable even though she should be feeling satisfied after their passionate night of love-making. Even when they'd been six years younger they'd never had such a night together.

She couldn't turn her back on such love. She had to trust it could continue. But she didn't want to look too far into the future. Making plans might jeopardise their happiness.

She touched his face gently. He opened his eyes and smiled as he reached out to draw her into his arms, skin against skin, breasts against his hard chest, damp bodies entwining with each other, exciting each other, arousing the senses so that they turned into one body that moved slowly, rapturously, until both of them cried out together as they climbed to the highest peak of their paradise…

* * *

Some time later, Tanya made a determined effort to escape from Manolis's arms and climb out of bed. She felt his restraining fingers on her thigh as her feet reached the floor.

"Manolis, I've got to go. I promised the boss I'd see this difficult patient at eight o'clock and I'm going to need a long soak in the bath before I can face the world."

He gave her a wry smile, "How about I help you bathe? That would make it much quicker for you and you could come back to bed now for a few minutes while I outline the patient's treatment."

She laughed as she shrugged into her robe. "The best plan is for you to go home in case your daughter arrives early."

"Spoilsport!" He pretended to sulk as he climbed out of bed and searched among the clothes strewn across the floor.

She gave one last fond look at the handsome hunk on his hands and knees.

"Duty calls," she said, as she slipped out of the door. Minutes later she heard him pattering down the stairs on his bare feet. She held her breath, expecting he would call into her bathroom to say goodbye. Her lips moistened at the thought of his lips on hers but she could hear his footsteps continuing to the ground floor.

Their idyll was over—for the moment.

CHAPTER SIX

HURRYING down the *kali strata* she still found time to pause and admire the view at the first corner after the initial descent from the upper town. She'd always stood right here since she'd been a child, holding her father's hand tightly so as not to slip on the well-worn cobbles.

The view of the harbour with the people on the boats beginning to wake up was spectacular as always. One tiny boat was making its way out to sea already. From this height, it looked like the blue boat she'd played with in her bath when she had been small.

She mustn't linger. She had a patient to see. He wasn't in any danger—she'd just checked again with the night sister but apparently he was being impatient about seeing her again.

A difficult patient, Night Sister had said. "You're telling me!" she'd replied, as she'd switched off her mobile. For a brief moment, she allowed herself to lift her eyes up to the horizon where an early morning mist had settled over the sea, making it difficult to figure out where the sea finished and the sky started.

And over there across the water on the hills of Turkey the morning glow of the newly risen sun had bathed the grass of the hills in a special light. Mmm, she loved this island. She was so glad she'd come home again, especially now that she'd made her peace with Manolis.

Moving swiftly down the steps, she realised it wasn't so much making peace with him as allowing herself to be honest. She hadn't really had time to get to know him during the weeks they'd been lovers in Australia. Yes, they'd had a wonderful heady, sexy relationship. But now, six years on, she was beginning to find out so much more about what this wonderful man was really about. She realised that she loved him so much still! She could never let him go again. They needed to rediscover each other and find out exactly what each of them had been through during the last six years.

She turned the corner at the bottom and made

her way through the wide terrace of tables outside a taverna where people were drinking their first coffee of the day.

"*Kali mera*, Tanya."

"*Kali mera*, good morning." She smiled as she greeted friends she remembered from her childhood.

She wended her way through the narrow streets, past the church and in through the front door of the hospital. It was still quiet. Nobody had dashed up to tell her she was needed yet. She checked with the night staff gathered round the nurses' station. Night Sister was giving her report to the newly arrived fresh faced, clean uniformed day staff.

She broke off to tell Tanya that nothing had changed since they'd spoken on the phone a short time ago. Alexander's condition had improved steadily throughout the night and he was asking to see her again now.

Tanya nodded. "Thanks, Sister. I'll go in and see him now."

Alexander's door was wide open, as it had been all night so that the night staff could keep a constant check. A young nurse was washing Alexander's face and hands, while her patient protested that he wasn't a baby. He didn't need all this fuss.

"Go away, Nurse. I want to speak to Dr Tanya."

He flapped a wet hand at the terrified nurse and indicated she should remove the bowl of soapy water from his bedside table.

"And close the door! Doesn't a man deserve a little privacy in this place? Do you realise who I am? In case it's escaped your notice, I'm Chairman of the Board of Governors at this hospital and I used to be the mayor of Ceres!"

He tried to raise himself up but flopped back against the pillows.

"Tanya, do I need all these tubes and things sticking in my hand?"

"That's your morphine line, Alexander. I told you last night before I left. You can press that little knob at the end of this tube if you are in pain and—"

"Oh, I've been doing that all night. I feel as high as a kite!"

The elderly patient gave a little giggle and held out a still damp hand towards Tanya, indicating that she should hold it in hers.

"I'm deeply grateful to what you and Manolis

did last night. I hope I wasn't too difficult with you in the interview, my dear. My wife is always telling me I'm cantankerous. But it's just my way of dealing with my own nerves, you know. I'm actually quite shy so I like to make people feel frightened of me—yes, I do! It means they won't walk all over me."

He broke off, looking confused. "I don't know why I'm telling you all this."

"It's the morphine. It loosens the tongue—a bit like alcohol."

"Oh, alcohol! I don't suppose you could smuggle in a small glass of ouzo, could you? Not even for medicinal purposes? No, I thought not."

"Give it a few days, Alexander. You've been through a big operation. We removed half your colon, your appendix, a couple of abscesses and—"

"You'll let me know when that pathologist man has done his tests, won't you, Tanya? I hope he gives me a clean bill of health. I don't want to die just yet. I enjoy life too much. Always have!"

"Now, I need to examine the wound."

"Never! Wait until Manolis comes. Lady

doctors have their place but I don't want you fishing around under my sheets."

He gave another uncharacteristic giggle. Tanya let go of his hand and checked the oxygen flow from the cylinder by his bed. "You won't need this much longer," she said, indicating the tube with the oxygen flowing into his nostrils.

"Thank goodness. Stop fiddling about, woman, and sit down on the bedside where I can look at you. Yes, you're beautiful like your mother and stubborn like your father. We got on so well, Sotiris and me, especially when I was mayor. Everybody thought we were deadly enemies but it was all an act, you know. We used to sink a few drinks after we'd been together in a public meeting, both taking different sides just for the hell of it. Well here the boy comes...at last! Close the door behind you, Manolis! I've just sent out for a bottle of ouzo so we can celebrate."

Manolis shot a glance at Tanya and she gave him a wry smile and a tiny nod of amusement.

"Alexander's been overdoing it on the morphine, Manolis. He—"

"Just listen to the woman! Get her out of here, my boy, before I drag her into my bed and show her who's boss around here." He started muttering incoherently. "Never could resist a pretty woman."

Manolis put his hand on Tanya's arm and spoke quietly. "I'll take over, Tanya, if you'd like to start on the patient round, please. I think this is our most difficult patient so I'll deal with the wound."

"I heard that, young man! I'm not senile yet. Get this oxygen tube out of my nose and be quick about it or…" He continued ranting to himself.

Manolis moved over to open the door for Tanya. She looked up into his eyes. For a few seconds neither of them spoke.

"Come and have a coffee in my office when you've finished your rounds, Doctor."

"I will, Manolis," she promised quietly.

"You make a lovely couple," came the now calm voice from the bed. "You'd better snap that beauty up before anybody else gets her. It was the same with her mother. I fancied her rotten but Sotiris got in there first. Mark my words, Manolis…"

Tanya closed the door on her patient's musings and headed for the obstetrics unit to check on Helene.

"Great to see you, Tanya!" Her friend was sitting in an armchair by her bed, cradling her newborn son. "I've just finished feeding so we can have a chat. I'll put Lefteris back in his cot."

"Let me do that, Helene. I need to check him out."

"Why?"

"Oh, just routine," Tanya said, as she placed the small baby on his cot and began her checks. "I'm on my rounds at the moment and I'll have to write a report on everybody I'm able to see so that the nurses know how to continue with their treatment today, what medication needs changing…that sort of thing."

"Well, can you put me down to go home? I'm getting bored in here and I'd love to be back at my grandmother's house with baby Lefteris's daddy."

"Well, as far as baby Lefteris is concerned, there are no problems. He's in excellent health. And as far as I can see from your chart, you've made an excellent recovery from your unscheduled home birth. You look great!"

Tanya settled the little boy in his cot and sat down on the edge of the bed. "I can't stay long. I've got to get round most of the patients and then spend the rest of the morning in Outpatients. Just wanted to see how you were doing."

"I really do want to go home!"

Tanya smiled. "Of course you do! It's only natural to want to be at home rather than be stuck in here. I'll recommend you're discharged today and if Manolis agrees…"

"Oh, thank you, Tanya! You know, I'm glad you're working with Manolis. When you were delivering my baby I could tell there was a spark between you two. It would be absolutely perfect if—"

"We're just a good team, that's all."

"Huh! Pull the other one!"

Tanya stood up. "I'll arrange for one of the nurses to go home with you later today to check that you settle in OK and have everything you need. Then a nurse will come in every morning for the next week to help you get used to being a mother. I think you'll be excellent."

"Can't wait to get started!"

Tanya smiled as she stood up. "I'll call in and see you later this morning when I've made the arrangements."

"So you're sure Manolis will accept your recommendation that I go home?"

"Of course! I mean, we seem to see eye to eye

on most of our professional responsibilities," she added hastily.

Helene grinned. "Sounds perfect to me. See you later, then."

Tanya continued on her rounds. She had two more patients to see in Obstetrics. The nurses had reported that one of these patients wasn't enjoying breastfeeding and found it difficult.

"My baby just doesn't suck, like she's supposed to," the young mother said. "She either falls asleep or starts screaming. The nurse had to give her a bottle last night to keep her quiet so we could all get some sleep."

"According to your chart, the nurse gave baby Rosa a bottle because she was worried she wasn't getting enough nourishment."

"Same thing!"

"Do you want to keep on with breastfeeding, Lana?" Tanya said gently.

The young mother pulled a face. "Not particularly. My mother told me I should breastfeed like all mothers on Ceres do. But to be honest I'd prefer to put her on the bottle so my husband can help with the feeding in the night. I need my sleep—I get really tired if I don't sleep enough."

"Well, let's give it another couple of days, shall we? You're staying with us till the end of the week because you had a hard time at the birth."

"It was awful, Doctor! I'm not going through that ever again. I thought I was going to die—and I actually wanted to when there was all this pain. Ugh!"

Tanya took hold of the young mother's hand. She'd skimmed through the notes and realised that her patient's blood pressure had been way too high and she'd been suffering from pre-eclampsia, a dangerous condition that, if untreated, could sometimes cause the death of the mother, the baby or both.

"You know Lana, for you to suffer as you did during your first labour must have been very frightening. It will take a while for you to regain your strength and feel as if you want to care for your baby."

"Actually, Doctor, I feel it was my baby's fault I've suffered so much. And it's hard to feel love for her when she was the cause of everything. She just cries all the time and I want to rest."

"You've had a very difficult time, Lana. Your beautiful little Rosa didn't ask to be born, did she? It's not her fault you had a bad time. You wanted her so much when you were strong. I'll get the nurses to see that you can rest more so that your strength returns. I'll ask them to give Rosa the occasional bottle but we'll also give you more help when you're trying to feed her."

"Thanks. I'd like that."

"You're so lucky to have such a healthy, beautiful baby. You might find you enjoy feeding her when you're feeling more rested and start getting to know Rosa. I'll come back and see you at the end of my morning."

By the end of her morning she was beginning to wish she hadn't promised to give so many patients a second visit. Fortunately, there were fewer outpatients than usual and those who came in weren't in a serious condition.

Amongst the patients she treated were a couple of tourists with mild sunstroke who only needed reassuring that if they stayed out of the sun till the end of their holiday, and applied the cream she gave them they would survive.

A small boy who'd fallen down in the school playground required a couple of stitches in his head and Tanya gave him a glass of milk and a biscuit because he said he hadn't had time for breakfast.

Another bigger boy required her to set his arm in a cast, having fallen from a tree and fractured his ulna. The four friends who'd come with him wanted to sign his cast immediately and then the patient wanted Tanya to sign it and the two nurses who'd helped her.

She hurried round the patients requiring second visits. As she came out of the orthopaedic unit where she'd given a second visit to reassure the young man who'd been admitted during the night with a fractured jaw that he was first on the list in Theatre that afternoon, she saw Manolis heading towards her down the corridor.

"We never did get that coffee," he said, looking down at her as they both paused.

"Later," she said.

"Much later. I've just scheduled Thomas for two o' clock. Has he been starved?"

"He's complaining he's had no food since yesterday evening. Difficult to tell what he says with that fractured jaw but—"

"He shouldn't even be trying to speak."

"That's what I told him. I gave him a notepad and a pencil so he can write instead of speaking."

"Good!" He paused. "I need an assistant in Theatre this afternoon."

"I thought you might."

"Let's take a break."

"Not now. Manolis, I need to—"

"Whatever it is, delegate it. We need a break together before we spend the afternoon and possibly the evening in Theatre."

She gave him a whimsical smile. "So I'm included in your schedule today, am I?"

"If I had my way..." He paused and took a deep breath while he stopped himself before he spoke his innermost thoughts. He mustn't say it—yet. He wanted to be absolutely certain of her feelings for him. He mustn't say that he wished she would be part of his whole life. He mustn't frighten her away again.

"Yes?"

"If I had my way, we wouldn't have so many emergency operations." He moved closer. "It would make life so much easier. But, then, we wouldn't have chosen to be doctors if we wanted an easy life."

He cleared his throat to get rid of the huskiness that had developed suddenly. Putting on his professional voice, he told her they would have a break together so that they could discuss the patient they were going to operate on that afternoon.

There was no one in the staff canteen when they arrived. A young waitress appeared from the kitchen and took their order. Manolis led the way to one of the small tables by the window, overlooking the harbour. He held the back of a chair until Tanya sat down on it. They looked at each other across the table.

Tanya had so many questions she wanted to ask Manolis about the six-year period in their lives when she'd tried to forget him. But now wasn't the time. Later, she hoped, there would be a real opportunity when they were alone and really off duty.

They discussed their patient, Thomas, while sipping their strong black Greek coffee as they waited for food to arrive.

"Apparently he was in that new nightclub on the edge of the harbour road. He was coming down from the roof terrace when he missed his footing and fell head first onto the ground floor.

He took the full force of his weight on his chin which, from the X-rays, looks as if it's shattered. I'll need to put a titanium plate in to keep the shards of bone from disseminating into the surrounding tissues, I think. But I'll decide exactly what needs to be done when I operate."

"Will you have to cut through the tissue at the front of the chin?"

"I'm going to try to approach it from the lower palate. As I say, it will become more obvious when I've got the patient under sedation."

He reached across the table and took her hand. She felt her body quiver imperceptibly at his touch. Even in the middle of a professional discussion her body could awaken with desire by the least physical contact.

"Thanks for agreeing to assist me. We work well together, don't we?"

She smiled, still very much aware of his fingers now stroking her hand. "It's my job to assist you when I'm needed."

The waitress had arrived with their food and was waiting to place it on the table. Manolis leaned back in his chair and simply looked across the table at the wonderful woman from his past who'd materialised in this unexpected way. He'd never thought he would get a second chance. He mustn't blow it this time.

Tanya looked at the Greek salad and kalimara they'd ordered. She watched as Manolis dressed it with oil and vinegar, before serving some onto her plate together with a few of the battered and deep-fried baby squid.

She smiled. "You remembered just how I like it."

"It was a long time ago but I seemed to remember automatically. It was that restaurant by the sea in Darling harbour, wasn't it?"

She laughed. "No, it was when we used to go to that Greek taverna by Bondi beach. Spend the whole day swimming. We always had Greek salad and kalimara because it was light enough for us to go in the water during the afternoon—after we'd had a short siesta under the trees."

"Yes, I remember now."

His eyes had taken on a distant look as his memory became nostalgic for those wonderful heady days of sun, sea, surf and sex with the most wonderful woman in the world. It could be like that again if…

"And now we're having the same meal because it's light enough to eat before a long afternoon in Theatre," Tanya said. "I'm enjoying the work here but I'm looking forward to the weekend to spend our off duty with you and Chrysanthe."

Manolis put down his fork and looked across the table. "There's been a change of plan, I'm afraid. We're expecting a large tourist vessel to be anchored off Ceres for the weekend. The tour company has informed us that the passengers are going to spend the whole weekend on the island." He hesitated. "I had to make the decision to cancel all weekend off duty."

She pulled a wry grin. "Oh, well, I suppose it was a wise decision. I'm disappointed but—"

"That's the problem with being in charge. I have to make wise but unpopular decisions. We'll get away one weekend soon. But now that the tourist season is in full swing, our off duty times will be a little unpredictable."

"I understand."

She did, she really did. But she longed to have more time with him. To sort out where they were both going together. A whole weekend together would have helped to cement this new uncertain relationship they were trying to sort out between work assignments.

She pushed her plate to one side and took the bold step of reaching across the table to take his hand in hers. "We'll just have to make the most of the time we can spend together."

He smiled across at her. "Always the pragmatic one. That's one of the things I like about you."

She smiled back. "Come on. We'd better get moving."

He glanced up at the clock. "Yes. The anaesthetist will be here in a few minutes and I want to fill him in on the patient's condition. He's got a history of high blood pressure…"

The operation was long and difficult but with the expertise of the surgical team it was a success. Manolis put two small titanium plates in the chin, which would ensure that the tiny fragments of bone were contained within their boundaries. The fractured jawbone required screws to hold it in place and he'd had to extract four molars, which were badly smashed and posed a danger at the back of the mouth.

Then he'd put four little hooks into the

patient's gums so that he could fix elastic bands around them to limit mobility of the mouth. Thomas was put on a high-protein-fluids-only diet for the next six weeks until the bone healed.

As she settled their patient in his bed after several hours, Tanya breathed a sigh of relief.

"Am I OK, Doctor?" Thomas murmured.

"You're going to be fine. But don't try to talk yet. There's a nurse sitting here beside you and she'll be there all night. So, anything you want, just scribble it on your notepad. I'll be in tomorrow morning to see you."

Her patient's grateful eyes told her all she needed to know. He was a tough young man and would pull through very well.

"Your girlfriend's just arrived and I've told her she can stay the night here so you've got a nurse and a girlfriend to take care of you. The morphine will help you to sleep."

Manolis held her hand as they walked up the *kali strata*.

"Let's stop here for a moment," Tanya said, feeling slightly breathless. "I always like to admire the view and catch my breath. It seems ages since I was here this morning. Such a difference now that Ceres harbour is bathed in moonlight. The twinkling lights on the boats and the tavernas—and the club where Thomas fell down the stairs last night. Poor Thomas! He's a good patient."

He turned and drew her into his arms. "And you're a very good doctor, Tanya."

She looked up into his eyes, seeing his tender expression that seemed so poignant in the moonlight.

"I always longed for the day when you would say that, Manolis."

His expression turned to one of surprise. "Did you?"

"That was one of the reasons I worked so hard to become a doctor. So that you would take me seriously."

"I've always taken you seriously."

"Yes, you have, since I grew up. But you did used to tease me as a child, didn't you?"

"Boys always believe girls are there to be teased. Your brother was just the same, wasn't he?"

"Exactly. But, yes, you're right. I shouldn't have taken it to heart as I did. But that's the way most young girls react."

"But you must admit I took you seriously when we met again and I realised you were grown up."

She smiled. "Yes, you certainly took me seriously then."

"I'd noticed you when you were a teenager but at that time the age gap was too much. But when I saw you that first time in Australia, I was absolutely blown away!"

He bent his head and kissed her lips as they parted to welcome him. For several idyllic seconds they remained locked in an exquisite embrace before the sound of footsteps threatened to disturb them.

"Let's go home," Tanya murmured as she tried to gather her strength for the final climb.

"Your place or mine?" he whispered.

Tanya was the first to waken. They'd both slept after making exquisitely wild passionate love on the soft feather mattress of her bed. It was a hot night and Manolis had thrown the sheet on to the floor where it lay entangled with their hastily discarded clothes. As she looked around her bedroom, with the early morning light filtering through the window, she felt glad that she'd suggested they sleep at her place last night. She loved waking up in her own bed with Manolis by her side.

She turned to look at him and her heart filled with love—real love this time, she realised. Had she experienced real love all those years ago when she had still been rather naïve about her emotions? Maybe. But not like she felt now.

He stirred beside her and opened his eyes, reaching for her, pulling her into his arms.

"Why are you looking so serious?

"I was just thinking how inexperienced I was when I moved in with you in Australia."

His eyes, so tender, locked with hers. "I didn't notice," he said huskily.

"Oh, I'm not talking about when we made love. That was just…just…"

"Wonderful? Out of this world?"

"Yes, it was, but emotionally I wasn't ready for the big commitment I was expected to make."

He leaned up on one elbow and stared down at her. "I hadn't realised that."

She swallowed hard. "When you asked me to marry you…I wasn't ready. It was such a big step. I wanted to be with you but…" Her voice trailed away.

"I'm sorry you felt…hassled?"

"Manolis, I didn't feel hassled. I just found that I had too many decisions to make all at once. My life had changed so completely in the space of a few weeks. When I told you I was pregnant and you proposed, I wondered if you were simply doing the dutiful thing and—"

"Of course I wasn't doing the dutiful thing! I wanted you to marry me so that we could bring up our child together!"

"And then again in the hospital after the miscarriage, I was in such a weakened state I couldn't think straight. I simply wanted time to sort out all my feelings." She took a deep breath. "If I could turn the clock back I think I would have done things differently. I wouldn't have asked you to leave like that. I just wanted you to go away for a while so I could sort out my confused feelings. I didn't think I might never see you again—"

He held her closer in his embrace. She was trying to hold back the tears. Between sobs she began again. "I remember the awful day, just a few weeks after I'd miscarried, when reality hit me and I realised how I'd mismanaged everything and you'd gone away for ever."

"I really thought that was what you wanted. Your mother had advised me not to contact you. I thought the best thing for everyone was if I started a new life and tried to forget you."

He was still holding her close as if to reassure himself that she wasn't going to vanish. This precious person, the only woman he'd ever really loved, was actually here with him and he had to tread carefully not to destroy his dreams.

"I was devastated when you sent me away," he said hoarsely as the memories came flooding back. "I don't even remember what I said to your mother when she advised me not to contact you. She asked me if I was OK, I remember, but the rest is a blur. I went straight back to the apartment and drank a beer, then another. Anything to dull the actual physical pain I was feeling. I'd lost my partner, my child, my whole life had changed in a matter of weeks and—"

"Darling, I'm sorry, I'm so sorry!" She stirred in his arms and raised her eyes to his. "If I'd been thinking normally I wouldn't have been so…so stupid as to break up what we had between us. What happened to you after that? What did you do the next day?"

"I wasn't fit for work. I wouldn't have let myself loose on the patients. I phoned in sick for a couple of days. Then I got a phone call from my old tutor in London—the one I told you about. He asked me if I'd thought about the post in London. I told him my circumstances; told him I was in a terrible emotional state. He advised me to resign and come straight over to London, told me I would feel better once I got away."

"So you went."

"There was nothing to hold me in Australia. I remember going through the interview, answering questions automatically, not even caring whether I got the job or not. I simply wanted the pain of losing you—and our child—to go away. And when I got the job, and started working, the pain started to ease. It wasn't so much physical then as a mental nagging at me that something wasn't right."

"But you had your new…girlfriend to comfort you."

"Yes, I suppose I had. But I couldn't help mentally comparing what I'd had with you, Tanya. I threw myself into my new job and it helped to be doing something I was trained to do, something that would help other people."

"Work always helps. I threw myself into my studies, worked hard at the practical work on the wards, tried not to think about what I'd lost, and little by little I returned to some sort of normality. Yes, the pain eased..." She swallowed hard as her voice began to falter.

"We've both suffered," she said softly as she started again. "Let's just take one day at a time. It's wonderful to be together again and..." Dared she say it? "And have a second chance at...at happiness together."

His lips sought hers. He'd wanted to kiss her as she struggled with her words, her emotions still confused, he could see. This time he wouldn't rush things. Wouldn't ask her to make decisions. His precious darling had to be treated gently, with great tenderness.

His kiss deepened as he felt himself become aroused once more. Tanya was responding, her beautiful body opening up to him. His breathing quickened.

Tanya cried out as they became one. Her body felt as if it was on fire with the sensual flames flickering through her. She climaxed over and over again until she lay spent with exhaustion, fulfilment and happiness in his arms...

CHAPTER SEVEN

ON THAT wonderful night when Manolis had taken her home after their lengthy session in Theatre, Tanya hadn't dreamed that it would be more than two weeks before the long-awaited day out on Manolis's boat. As she hurriedly packed a small bag with towel and spare bikini—she was already wearing her favourite white one under her jeans—her thoughts drifted back to that exquisite night they'd spent together.

It had certainly been a turning point in their relationship. She remembered how he'd carried her up the narrow stairs to her bedroom. They'd laughed at the romantic gesture that had always made them giggle when they'd been living together in his tiny apartment in Sydney.

The people who owned the apartment had been Greek and had built a small mezzanine floor with a moussandra—a raised platform—for the bed.

Manolis had so often insisted on carrying her up the small staircase when it had been obvious to both of them that they were going to fall on to the bed and make love.

He'd carried her upstairs so gently when he'd come to terms with the fact that she was expecting their baby. For a few days after she'd first told him she could tell he was shocked but it hadn't taken long before he'd said he was looking forward to being a father. He'd insisted on cooking supper for them that evening, she remembered, making her sit with her feet up on the sofa.

Afterwards he'd scooped her up in his arms and carried her carefully up the stairs.

"Our first child," he'd said as he'd laid her gently on the bed, treating her as if she were made of Dresden china. "I shall carry you upstairs from now on."

She'd laughed, telling him when she got as big as a house she wouldn't hold him to it. But that hadn't happen anyway because she hadn't got very far on the motherhood road…

She zipped up her bag and told herself she wasn't going to continue that train of thought. Their present relationship was sailing along beautifully now. She wouldn't allow herself to dwell on the past or the future. Only the present was what she cared about when she was with Manolis. They'd both established that fact when they'd made love a couple of weeks ago. It was as if they'd never had that six-year split. Their bodies were so tuned to each other's that…

She drew in her breath and shivered with re-membered sensual passion. It had been the most wonderful night of her life—until the next night and the next night…

"Are you up there, Tanya?" came the recog-nisable voice of Chrysanthe.

Tanya's door was always open and Chrysanthe often wandered in when she knew that Tanya was home.

"Yes, come on up, *agapi mou*. I'm nearly ready."

"Daddy says we've got to go soon. He was using his cross voice so I think he means now."

The little girl arrived panting at the top of the stairs that led straight into Tanya's bedroom. She held out her arms for a hug. Tanya lifted her up and hugged her, revelling in the clean smell of soap and shampoo. She sat her down on the edge of the bed.

"Let me look at you, Chrysanthe. I love the new shorts!"

"Daddy bought them ages ago because I was sad we couldn't go out in the boat. He said it was because you both had to work every day because the tourists kept on breaking their bones or cutting their skin or getting sick."

"That's very true. But we've got a whole day off today."

"Why do the tourists make such a lot of work for you and Daddy? In the winter when it's just the people who live on the island you won't have to work so hard, will you? You and Daddy will be able to look after me properly, won't you?"

"What's that about looking after you properly?" came a whimsical deep voice from down below. "If you girls don't get a move on, I'll have to go without you."

Manolis took the stairs two at a time and stood at the top, half in and half out of her bedroom. It was as if his heart missed a beat when he saw the two people most precious to him. Together, just like mother and daughter. Only they weren't. They should have been if… Don't go there!

"What was that I heard you say, Chrysanthe?

You don't think we look after you properly when the tourists are here? Are you trying to say you feel neglected?"

He was using a jocular tone but his daughter's words had reinforced the worry he had about the way his precious child was being brought up.

"What does neglect mean?"

Manolis looked across at Tanya as if he wanted her to help him out.

"Well it's a bit difficult," she began cautiously. "Would you like to spend more time with Daddy?"

"Yes, and you as well, Tanya. You're like my mummy now, aren't you?"

Tanya's eyes locked with Manolis's, both of them now pleading for help in a delicate situation.

It was Tanya who spoke first to ease the tension. "Well, I help to look after you, Chrysanthe, but you've already got a mummy in England, haven't you?"

"Yes, but you could be my mummy here on the island, couldn't you? I'd like that."

Manolis could feel his heartstrings pulling. He noticed that Tanya's eyes were moist. She was holding back her tears. He wanted to draw her into his arms, tell her he loved her, ask her to become the second mother to his daughter, make some more babies of their own…

Thoughts rushed through his head about all the things he wanted to do but didn't dare suggest. He had to take it more slowly this time round. He'd rushed her the last time when he'd asked her to marry him after only a few weeks together. They needed time to simply enjoy being together again.

"I enjoy looking after you and being with you, Chrysanthe," Tanya said carefully, deliberately avoiding Manolis's eyes.

"I think we should set off now," Manolis said briskly. "The harbour's getting busier by the minute and I've always found it hard to extricate my boat when the place is full of tourists."

Tanya rolled her eyes at Chrysanthe as she scooped her up into her arms. "Now he tells us!"

Chrysanthe dissolved into a fit of giggles. "I'll drive the boat, Daddy! I know how to do it. Uncle Lakis showed me. You just put your hand on the steering-wheel and—"

"OK, child genius," Manolis said, taking her from Tanya's arms and beginning the descent of the stairs. "I'll let you have a go with the boat when we're safely at the tiny island where we're going to have lunch."

"Can we have a barbecue?"

"Of course! But only if you help me catch a nice big fish."

It was, they all agreed, one of the biggest fish that had ever been caught on Ceres. Well, at least on the small rocky island where they'd moored the boat. It had taken Manolis and Chrysanthe only half an hour before it had taken their bait and got hauled in. Chrysanthe and Tanya had then spent a long time swimming and playing in the water while Manolis had gutted the fish and put it on the barbecue he'd rigged up at the edge of the sea.

"When's the food ready, Daddy?" Chrysanthe had called several times, only to be told it wouldn't be long but he needed a swim before he served it. They were finally all able to swim together, amid a lot of laughter and splashing about. As they came out of the water, the three of them holding hands with Chrysanthe in the middle, Manolis glanced across at Tanya, his heart full of love for the family that seemed to have emerged so suddenly.

She swallowed hard as she looked at him. Was this what parenting was about, would be about if only she could commit to Manolis again? But did he still want her? He needed her…yes…but…

"Smell that wonderful fish!" Manolis called, clambering back up the rocks to rescue the precious fish from the grill of the barbecue where an inquisitive goat was wondering if it dared brave the fire.

Manolis told the girls to sit down so that he could serve them and they crouched by the fire, accepting delicious offerings of fish, Greek salad and crusty bread, washed down with wine or fresh lime juice in Chrysanthe's case.

Tanya stretched out on her sandy towel and chewed on the delicious piece of fish that Manolis had just handed to her on the end of his fork. She'd taken it with her fingers and popped it into her mouth.

"Mmm, delicious! What is it?"

"It's some kind of *psari*, rather like tuna—I don't know it's name in English." They were talking in Greek, as they often did.

"It's *psari*, fish," Chrysanthe said.

Manolis smiled. "We know it's fish, darling, but we were wondering exactly what kind."

Chrysanthe shrugged. "I'll look it up in my picture book of fish when we get back. I often have to translate words when we're having our English lesson at school because my teacher says I'm bi-biling…something."

"Bilingual," Tanya supplied.

"What does it mean?"

"It means you can speak two languages."

"Can't everybody?"

"They often can if they've got one English parent and one Greek parent. That's why I'm bilingual."

"Just like me!" Chrysanthe snuggled closer, oblivious to the fact that she was putting her sticky fingers on Tanya's towel.

"Have you had enough fish, you two?"

"Absolutely! That was wonderful!"

"Would madam care for dessert?"

Tanya picked up a flat pebble and pretended to study the menu. "I'll have the crème caramel."

"I'm afraid it's off. Would madam settle for an orange?"

"If it's freshly picked from the tree."

Manolis reached up and pretended to take an

orange from the branch overhanging their shady spot.

Chrysanthe had gone past giggling and was laughing loudly now. "Daddy, you and Tanya are so funny," she spluttered. "I like it when you don't have to work. You're much more fun. I'd like to live on this island, wouldn't you?"

"Oh, you'd get bored eventually," Manolis said as he rummaged through the hamper in search of the oranges.

Tanya stretched out on her towel, Chrysanthe having suddenly decided to run down to the edge of the sea in search of some more shells.

She looked up at the blue cloudless sky and then glanced across at the smart new motorboat bobbing on the water nearby. It had been such fun as they'd left the harbour far behind and Manolis had been able to speed along over the waves. Chrysanthe had shouted with delight when they'd reached their little island. It was little more than a few rocks surrounded by sand but Chrysanthe had announced that it was their own special island from now on.

"We're completely alone on this island, aren't we?" she breathed as she took the orange that

Manolis was handing to her. "It's like playing at Robinson Crusoe. I agree with Chrysanthe. I'd like to live here and eat nothing but fish and oranges."

He leaned across her and kissed her gently on the mouth. She responded, but not as much as she would have done if they'd been alone. Glancing across at the small figure by the water, she saw that Chrysanthe was fully occupied in gathering shells, which they would soon have to inspect. She allowed herself the luxury of parting her lips and savouring the moment. Her body was stirring with desire. She pulled away as gently as she could so as not to destroy the delicious ambience they'd created.

"Mmm, it's so peaceful."

"Utter bliss," Manolis said, his fingers lightly moving down her arm. "I'm having difficulty controlling myself."

"Me too!"

"Are you free this evening?"

"I'll have to check my diary first."

"Cancel everything," he murmured, drawing her closer.

"I might just do that," she murmured, before dragging herself away and holding out her hand to be pulled up. "It's time we gave some quality time to our little darling."

The word "our" wasn't lost on Manolis as he drew Tanya to her feet. "Is that how you think of her?"

She hesitated. "I'm afraid it is now," she said, slowly.

"Don't be afraid, Tanya. Enjoy this feeling of family that we now have. We're all so close and—"

"Daddy, Tanya, come and see this little fish in the water. It's nibbling my toes, come and see it."

They inspected the fish, before going further out into the bay to swim. Tanya was relieved to find that Chrysanthe swam like a fish. There was no need to worry about her, although she and Manolis swam one on each side of her.

When they came out of the sea Chrysanthe stretched out on the sand under the trees in their picnic spot at the edge of the shore where the sand turned to rocks. "I'm quite sleepy," she murmured as she curled into a ball, closed her eyes and drifted off to sleep like a baby.

Manolis took hold of Tanya's hand. "I'm quite sleepy too," he murmured as he gently took her to one side of the sleeping child and moved across to a shady spot where they could still keep an eye on Chrysanthe.

"You're so wicked," Tanya said as he drew her down on to the sand beside him.

"I know." His fingers toyed with the strap of her bikini top.

"No," she whispered, her hand covering his. "Not in front of your daughter."

He gave her a wry grin. "Prude!"

"I'm not! And you know it. It's just that if she were to wake up she'd be so shocked. Oh, I don't know. It's all part of learning about being a parent."

She stopped, knowing she'd said more than she meant to. "And I'm not even a parent so...I know my place in this family. I'm just a friend."

"My darling, you're more than a friend and you know it. You mean...such a lot to me. Now that you've come back into my life it's so natural that you're part of the family. That's how Chrysanthe thinks of you anyway."

"But I'm not part of the family!"

He drew her closer and kissed her gently as he felt her shoulders shaking. She was crying now.

He didn't know how to handle this. He hadn't known how to handle her when she'd lost their baby. She'd cried and he'd felt so useless—just as he felt now. The last time she'd cried in his arms he'd begged her to marry him so he could take care of her. But she'd pushed him away, told him she wanted to be alone.

So this time he remained silent. Held her until the sobs subsided, kissed her gently on the lips and then released her from his embrace.

She was calm now as she turned to him. "I'm sorry. I just felt a bit strange, that's all. It sort of brought back memories I want to forget. I'm happy with the way we are now, aren't you, Manolis?"

"I'm glad you came back into my life," he said carefully.

He was holding himself in check now. One word too many and the whole bubble of his happiness would burst.

"We've been through such a lot together and now…I just don't know how to handle the parent thing." She looked into his eyes so earnestly locked with hers. "How do you think Victoria will feel when she finds out Chrysanthe regards me as a mother figure here?"

"Victoria was never very maternal. She was anxious to get on with her career and insisted on employing a nanny right from day one. I used to bring Chrysanthe out to Ceres as often as I could because she was so happy here. She adores my mother and her cousins. When she was about three she asked if we could come and live here with Grandma. That was when I handed in my notice in London and bought the house on the island. Victoria's reaction was one of relief. Oh, don't get me wrong. She loves Chrysanthe but she doesn't give out that natural warmth that she needs—like you do. You're doing magnificently, especially as you're not a parent. I mean…"

"I know what you mean. I should have been a parent. We should have been parents together…"

"Darling!" He held her close again as her sobs renewed.

She rubbed her eyes with the back of her hand. "Hey, I'd better snap out of this. I don't know what came over me. Haven't cried so much since…well, a long time ago, you know."

"I know." His tone was very gentle, so scared to break up the newfound bond that was developing between them. "Look, we've both been there, done that and survived." He cleared his throat. "So, how about we have a party tonight to celebrate?"

"A party?"

He reached forward again at the alarmed expression on her face. "Not a party party. Just the two of us at my place. A bottle of champagne—oh, yes, we can now get champagne on Ceres. Thing have changed since you lived here."

"Well, I certainly was never allowed to drink the imported champagne at any of the family weddings."

"You were too young." He ran his fingers through her hair. "But you started to grow up and I remember looking at you when you were sixteen or seventeen and thinking if you were only a few years older, you would be perfect for me."

"Did you really?" She snuggled against him.

"Of course I did! So did all my friends. You were absolutely gorgeous—but completely unaware how attractive you were."

"I wish I'd known I was attractive. I was so caught up in the idea of proving myself clever enough to be a doctor like my dad, my brother and you that I never wore make-up or short skirts or anything like that. Relationships with the opposite sex were all pushed to one side."

A thoughtful expression flitted across his face. "That might account for a lot of things."

"Like what?"

She lay back in his arms, looking up through the leaves above her head. A large heron was flying above her. It skimmed above her head, swooping down towards the sea before expertly lifting a small fish into its jaws and flying away over the calm blue waters.

"Like why it took all my powers of persuasion to get you to move in with me in Sydney. You'd grown up to be a beautiful young woman by then but you still seemed completely unaware of the fact that you were enormously fanciable."

She grinned mischievously. "Oh, I was totally aware. I was just fed up with playing the little-woman bit. I'd realised that at long last friends and family took me seriously. At last I'd got the power to be independent. And I wasn't going to surrender all that so easily."

He swallowed hard. "So when you surrendered to me, as you put it, it was a kind of testing time, was it?"

"It was a wonderful time in my life…while it lasted."

"And now…back to the present. Will you come to my party tonight?" he said. "I promise, we won't talk about the future."

She smiled. "You know me so well."

He gave her a wry grin. "I'm beginning to."

"Then I'd love to come to your party."

She glanced across at Chrysanthe who was sitting up now, looking around her, slightly bewildered.

"Tanya! Daddy! Let's go swimming again, shall we?"

Tanya went in through the open door and sat down in Manolis's small kitchen.

"I'm here!" she called as her eyes became accustomed to the twinkling candles on the kitchen table and took in the champagne holder full of ice, waiting for the bottle, which was obviously chilling in the fridge.

"Come on up! I'm in the bedroom."

"Is that wise?"

"Probaby not, but come up anway."

He was standing at the top of the staircase. He

was wearing one of the faded sarongs they'd bought from an Indonesian trader when they'd been in Australia. He looked like an Olympic athlete, every muscle of his well-honed body hard and ready for action. She stood up. In a couple of seconds he reached the ground floor and drew her into his arms.

He nuzzled her hair. "I've been waiting all day for this moment."

"Me too!"

"So you didn't enjoy our day on our island?"

"It was wonderful!" She raised her head for his kiss. "But like a tired non-parent, I'm ready for some adult fun."

"Adult fun! Well you've come to the right place." He bent down and blew out the candles. "Just in case we don't get down here for an hour or so."

He reached into the fridge, took out the bottle of champagne and dumped it into the champagne cooler. Holding this in one hand, he scooped her up into his arms with the other and made for the stairs.

This time when they made love it was exquisitely tender, each body dovetailing into the other as if they'd never been apart. He held her so close, so much part of him, so loved, that she thought she had never known such happiness.

And when she reached the pinnacle of her climax she cried out at the impossible wonder of being once more with the man she'd loved first in her life and maybe would go on to love… for…for a long time.

As she lay back against the pillows and looked into his eyes she knew she'd really come home this time. She would give up everything for him, she was ready now. She'd gone through the independent bit. It was possible to be a wife, a mother even and still have it all with a man like Manolis. If she could only convey this to him now. He'd asked her before and been turned down. Would he ever ask her again?

He stroked her cheek, his eyes locking with hers. "Why so serious now?"

"Am I serious?"

"If I didn't know you so well I'd say there was something important on your mind. You're going to make an announcement."

She hesitated. He wouldn't like it if she

proposed to him. He really wouldn't. He was this macho Greek man, steeped in centuries of male dominance. The last thing she should do was make the first move—even if she wanted to. After the way she'd treated him in Australia she was probably the last woman on earth he'd ever propose to. Anyway, why was she so suddenly getting soft about marriage? She didn't need to be married, did she? Her love for Manolis was strong enough to survive anything now.

"No, I'm not going to make an announcement," she improvised. "Except to say I'm starving and about to call room service."

He kissed the tip of her nose before reaching for the champagne bottle on his bedside table.

"Room service coming right up."

As he was deftly pouring the fizzy liquid into her glass and handing it to her, the thought occurred that it could be a good time to pop the question uppermost in his mind. But even as the thought came into his mind he dismissed it.

This woman would never surrender her independence. He could feel that she loved him again now but anything more was pure fantasy.

He would settle for the present, wonderful as

it was, and leave the conventional ideas to other couples. Tanya still needed her freedom and he had to respect that.

CHAPTER EIGHT

"I'm going to see Mummy in England next week, Tanya—my English mummy—not you. Daddy told me this morning. But you'll still be here when I get back, won't you? You'll never leave me, will you?"

Tanya lifted the small excited girl into her arms and kissed her soft cheek. The beautiful, sensitive dark brown eyes—just like her father's—were pleading with her to stay for ever. How could she answer such a poignant request? Over the summer weeks she'd grown so close to Chrysanthe, to love this child as if she were her own. But how could she predict what the future held for Manolis and herself at this delicate stage in their relationship? She was going to do all she could to ensure that they continued to trust each other more and more but she still wasn't sure how Manolis felt about a permanent relationship now.

She swallowed hard. "Of course I'll be here when you get back from England." That was definitely true.

Chrysanthe looked around proudly as she saw her other small friends greeting their mothers at the school gate. A couple of her friends had already asked if the pretty doctor lady was her mother. She'd wanted to say yes, but she knew that would have been a naughty lie so she'd had to tell the truth. So she'd told them she had two mummies—one in England and one in Ceres.

Tanya was putting her down on the ground now. That was good. Lots of her friends had seen her being greeted by her wonderful Ceres mummy.

She grabbed hold of Tanya's hand and called goodbye to her nearest friend, who'd kept on all day in school about her new baby brother. She must find out about the possibility of a new baby brother or sister for herself. She wasn't quite sure how it worked. It was something to do with mummies and daddies getting together to plant a seed somewhere but her English mother had told her it probably wouldn't happen till her daddy got married again.

She squeezed Tanya's hand tightly. She'd have

to work on that one. Grown-ups could be so difficult about things that seemed so simple. If Katia's mummy could get a baby brother for Katia, why couldn't one of her mummies get one for her?

"I told my friends you were my Ceres mummy." Chrysanthe looked up at Tanya as she skipped along beside her, anxious to see her reaction. You never knew with grown-ups. They had funny ideas about what was proper and what wasn't.

Tanya stopped walking for a moment and looked down at the adorable little girl. She loved her to bits but she could be so precocious at times. They'd reached the section of the *kali strata* where the steps became steeper before the final slog to the top. She looked away for a moment, trying to draw inspiration from the beautiful view of the harbour and the hills beyond, but nothing came into her head to resolve the situation.

"Did you, darling?" She knew this was no resolution but she had to say something when Chrysanthe was looking up at her so anxiously, obviously seeking approval.

"Well, they wanted to know if you were my

mummy so I had to tell them you were my second mummy," Chrysanthe said quickly. "That wasn't a lie, was it?"

Tanya wasn't sure what to say now. She'd had a busy day in hospital and questioning from Chrysanthe was hard work right now. Especially when you weren't a parent! If only Manolis were here.

She'd left him in Theatre reconstructing a mangled leg. Their patient had somehow managed to get caught up in a two-car collision and been shunted by a car with dodgy brakes. Manolis had taken her to one side just before he'd started the operation and told her it was time she went off duty. He would get assistance from Yannis, their new doctor who'd trained in Athens but had recently returned to Ceres, where he'd been born. He'd applied for the temporary post during the tourist season that they'd recently advertised.

"I took him on for the season because he has excellent references. He comes from a good family here on Ceres. His wife died a couple of years ago and he's decided to make a break from their life together in Athens. Anyway, I'd like to give him a chance to show what he can do," he whispered. "If he's anything as good as you are…"

"Flattery will get you everywhere, Doctor," she told him. "I must admit that the thought of a long hot bath would—"

"Well, actually, I wondered if you could pick up Chrysanthe from school?"

"I knew there'd be a catch in it! Only joking! I'd love to. Haven't seen her for a couple of days."

"That's what she told me this morning. She asked if you could pick her up like a proper mummy."

Tanya had groaned. "She's obsessed with mummies at the moment."

"I think it's because she's off to London next week. And also she likes her friends to think you're her mummy."

She brought herself back to the current dilemma as Chrysanthe repeated the question that had to be answered now. "It wasn't a lie when I said you were my Ceres mummy, was it?"

"If that's how you think of me…then…"

"Oh, thank you, Tanya! I do love you!"

"And I love you too, Chrysanthe."

Tears were pricking her eyes as she held onto the hot, sticky hand that was tightly clinging to hers. She sniffed and wiped a tissue over her eyes with her other hand before they continued the final section of the steep steps.

"Now, what shall we do when we get back home?"

"Your home? We're going to your home, aren't we? I like your house. Can we do some baking like we did last time I came to see you? We could make some more of those little jam tarts."

"Yes, we could."

Tanya took a deep breath as she realised she must draw on her inner reserves of strength. She had to keep going at the end of this long, tiring day. She couldn't disappoint Chrysanthe.

By the time Chrysanthe had mixed the flour with butter and water, plunging her little fingers into the dough-like substance, they were both laughing. Tanya was reinvigorated and had completely forgotten she was tired as she joined in the excitement of producing the tarts, which they were planning to eat as soon as they were ready.

"Can I invite my cousins round to help us eat them?"

Tanya wiped a damp kitchen towel over

Chrysanthe's sticky hands. "Of course. The more the merrier!"

Chrysanthe reached up her hands and put them round Tanya's neck so that she could pull down her face for a kiss on the cheek. "I'll go and see who's with Grandma today. Don't go away, will you, Tanya?"

"No, I won't go away…"

The following week, when it was time for Chrysanthe to go to London, Tanya felt sad that she wasn't going to see her little surrogate daughter for two whole weeks. She placed the chicken casserole she'd made on the kitchen table and looked across at Manolis, who'd come round for supper.

"I'm really going to miss her, you know."

She picked up the large soup ladle and put a generous helping on Manolis's plate.

"Mmm, this smells delicious. You always could make a good casserole." He put down his spoon and looked directly into her eyes. "Did I tell you I'm going to stay in London for three days when I take Chrysanthe to Victoria's house?"

She sat down and busied herself with the wax

dripping onto the table from one of the candles she'd lit to make the little kitchen seem romantic.

"No, I don't believe you did," she said nonchalantly. "I rather thought you were coming straight back."

"Well, Victoria says it's time I got to know Toby, her boyfriend. She's moved into his big house near Hyde Park. Apparently, it was his idea that I should stay until Chrysanthe settles in."

"Sounds a very understanding sort of person."

She tried to swallow a small spoonful of chicken and look as if she was unaffected by the idea of Manolis spending three days in London with his ex-wife.

"He's a retired cardiac surgeon, I believe."

"Retired? So he's older than Victoria?"

"Oh, yes. He's got grown-up children and a couple of small grandchildren. His wife left him for a younger man, I believe. Victoria told me they started off having a platonic friendship and then one thing led to another. I don't think it's a passionate love affair but it seems to suit them both."

Manolis bent his head and applied himself to the casserole, hoping they could now drop the subject. He'd explained what was going to happen but Tanya seemed concerned.

Tanya swallowed her spoonful of chicken and tried to think of a different subject than the one now uppermost in her mind. Was she jealous or was it just that she couldn't bear the thought of being without Manolis for the best part of four days?

She cleared her throat. "How do you know all this…er…stuff about Victoria?"

"Oh, she often phones to ask about Chrysanthe…how she's getting on at school, that kind of thing… May I have some more of this fantastic casserole?"

"Help yourself."

"You've hardly eaten anything. Let me serve you."

"No, thanks. I'm OK. But you go ahead."

There was an awkward silence for a while as Manolis finished his food and Tanya toyed with hers.

After a while she spoke. "What time do you leave tomorrow?"

"The boat leaves at seven."

He reached across the table and took hold of

her hand. "What is it, darling? You don't look your usual self tonight."

"I'm tired, that's all." She picked up her plate and took it over to the sink. "I think I'll have an early night—"

He rose slowly, languidly from his seat and came round the table, a seductive smile on his face as he stood looking down at her. "How about I join you?"

She looked up into his dark liquid eyes and thought he'd never looked more desirable.

He drew her into his arms and kissed her tenderly, first on the lips and then on her neck. She felt his hands undoing the top button of her blouse and her body began to quiver with the renewed passion that always rose when they were close together.

"Why not?" she whispered.

Their love-making was tinged with a certain sadness that night. As Tanya revelled in their intimate embrace afterwards, legs entwined together, she was feeling much more relaxed than she had done at the supper table.

"You said you would miss Chrysanthe," he

whispered, his hands gently running through her hair. "Are you going to miss me?"

"You know I am!"

"I don't know unless you tell me. I never know what you're thinking about me. I never did understand what goes on in that pretty little head of yours."

He leaned on his elbow and looked down into her eyes. The moon was so bright that they hadn't put the light on, both having agreed wordlessly that it was more romantic to make love by moonlight.

"I shall miss you a lot," she said quietly. "Just like I did in Australia after you left me."

"I left because you told me to go."

"I know. I was confused. As I told you before, I thought your proposal was simply you being dutiful. I didn't realise you…had strong feelings for me. Yes, we'd always enjoyed making love together but a lifetime commitment was too big for me to contemplate. You know I'd do things differently now, don't you? I hope I've made that clear if you're in any doubt about it."

She looked up at him thinking he'd never looked more handsome, more desirable. His dark rumpled hair was partly obscuring his face but she'd memorised his seductive expression over and over again as they'd made love. She wanted to be able to conjure up his image in her mind during the time when he wasn't with her.

She knew, without a shadow of a doubt, that she wanted to move their relationship on a level. If he were to propose to her now...If only he would! Surely he could read her thoughts. Surely she was making it obvious that she wanted their relationship to be permanent this time round.

He watched the worried expression that was flitting across her face. Something was disturbing her. Was she still scared of commitment? She'd always been a strong, independent person who needed to be as free as a bird. If he were to voice his innermost desire to make her his wife, would she clam up and go all cold on him again? Better to enjoy the relationship they had now than risk losing her again. She'd said she would do things differently this time, but had she really thought about the consequences, the lifetime commitment?

A rasping sigh escaped his lips as he ran a hand through his hair, pulling it back from his eyes so that he could appreciate how beautiful, how infinitely desirable but how totally inaccessible she was.

"Why the big sigh?"

He took a deep breath. "I was thinking it was time…it was time I finished my packing."

"Packing! I'll set my alarm. You can't do it in the middle of the night!"

"Oh, but I can!" He was already out of bed, pulling on his trousers. "No, don't get up. You need your sleep. I'll see myself out. Goodnight, darling. Sleep well. I'll phone while I'm away."

He was leaning down, taking her in his arms for a final kiss. He really was leaving! She felt a moment of panic—not like when he left her before but something akin to that.

And then he was gone.

She buried her face in the pillow but she didn't cry. Her eyes were totally dry as she closed them and forced herself to remember that he was only going away for three nights. Three whole nights when he wouldn't come round from his house next door, take her in his arms, hold her through the night in his embrace…

The tears were beginning to make themselves felt behind her closed eyelids. She didn't want to cry. It was her own fault that their relationship had reached stalemate. She hadn't cried the first time round when she'd asked him to leave.

Yes, her hormones had been all over the place after her miscarriage. But at that stage in her life she hadn't realised that it would pass and she would arrive at the other side of the tragedy longing for the only man in the world who could help her put her life back together again.

She sat up in bed and reached for the box of tissues on the bedside table, rubbing her damp face vigorously. The moon had gone behind a cloud and her bedroom was dark now. She switched on the bedside lamp and leaned back against the pillows, staring up at the ceiling.

Supposing she were to bring up the subject of marriage with him? Couples sometimes just seemed to agree on marriage nowadays. It didn't seem to matter who brought up the idea. She'd met couples who'd just sort of drifted into marriage by common consent. But not with the background that Manolis had! Born here on Ceres, he was steeped in the importance of family. The man was the head of the family. When he was planning to take a wife and start his own family it was he who did the running, he who proposed to the woman of his choice.

He was macho through and through! As a boy he'd been made to feel how important he was. His mother, grandmother, sisters had all spoiled him, as was right and proper with the male of the species. With a family background like that he wouldn't dream of breaking the rules of life that had been set out long before his birth.

But she loved him more than life itself now. So it was up to her to make it clear—in a subtle way, of course—that she'd changed, that she was waiting for him to propose again and this time her answer would definitely be yes, yes, a thousand times yes!

When she got into hospital next day she went straight to see Patras, the patient who'd been involved in the car crash the previous day. She'd promised Manolis last night that she'd give him extra attention while he was away in London.

The doctor leaning over the patient's bed, inspecting the leg which Manolis had operated on, turned to look at her as she joined him.

"*Kali mera.* You must be Tanya. Manolis told

me you would be here to help me while he's in London. I'm Yannis. I've recently come over from Athens and joined the team as a temporary doctor for the rest of the tourist season."

He smiled and held out his hand. She felt a firm grip as she reciprocated the introduction, thinking all the while what a pleasant addition he was to the medical team. Tall and dark and definitely handsome, he would probably find the single members of the hospital staff fawning all over him! And some of the married ones too!

But not herself. She was so head over heels in love that she couldn't imagine how any woman could contemplate cheating on her man.

He was a consummate professional and a gentleman—she could see that by the deferential way he stepped back to allow her to examine their patient. He waited as she washed her hands at the sink close to the bed. When she turned round she saw something she hadn't noticed before—the aura of sadness that surrounded him in spite of his welcoming smile.

She remembered Manolis saying something about the new doctor having lost his wife a couple of years ago. How long did it take for someone to recover from the death of a loved one? Perhaps you never did.

He handed her the patient's notes. "I assisted Manolis yesterday in Theatre," he said quietly. "It was a difficult operation. These are the X-rays."

Yannis slotted them into the screen on the wall and switched on the light. She could see the shattered tallus had been pushed upwards and had impinged on the tibia, causing it to shatter into several fragments. She could see where Manolis had inserted screws and pins to hold the tibia in place so that it could, hopefully, knit together and form part of a viable leg when the healing process took over. Manolis had told her that Patras was basically a fit young man whose bones were very strong. It was only the intensity of the impact with part of the engine of the car he had been driving that had caused the bone to shatter.

Yannis removed the top part of the cast covering the leg so that Tanya could see the extent of the injury.

"How are you feeling, Patras?"

The young man grinned. "Better than I was. How long will I have to stay in, Doctor? Only

I've got a hot date with a new girlfriend tonight and I'd rather like to get out. Couldn't you just give me some crutches and I'll be on my way?"

Tanya straightened up and looked down at her patient. "I'd love to be able to say it was that easy, Patras, but the fact is we're going to have to keep you in for a few days. At least until Dr Manolis gets back from London. This is a complicated break that's going to take—"

"When will Manolis be back?"

"In three days. He'll probably keep you in for a week at least, I'm afraid. So my advice is to phone your girlfriend and see if she wants to come in and see you. Have you got a mobile with you?"

Patras pulled a wry grin. "It sank in the harbour along with my car. I got dragged out just in time. The driver of the other car—the one that was too far over on my side of the road and made me swerve—escaped without a mark on him."

"I'll bring you a landline and plug it into that socket by your bedside table," Tanya said. "We'll be taking you down to X-Ray soon. Manolis has requested new X-rays for his post operational records."

"Well, that's something to look forward to," the

young man quipped. "I'm going to get so restless when I'm in here."

"I'll get you a television," Yannis said. "There's a football match you might you might like to watch this afternoon."

"Great! Thanks very much, Doctor."

CHAPTER NINE

SOMEHOW she got through the three nights and four days knowing that Manolis was living it up in London with his ex-wife. Well, that's what it seemed like to her! He'd phoned every day to give her an account of what was happening there but the phone calls were brief and to the point.

He seemed to be having a great time. Victoria's husband was a good host and entertained them well in the evenings. Mostly, he had "things to do, meetings with friends and colleagues during the day" so it was left to Victoria to take them around London seeing the sights and generally making sure that Chrysanthe was happy.

And it certainly sounded as if Victoria was making sure her ex-husband was happy. He always sounded exhilarated, relaxed. He never told her he was missing her. But why should he miss her? He'd spent six years without her. What was four days and three nights?

On the fourth day, the day he was coming back to Ceres, she lay in bed staring at the ceiling, trying to contain her excitement but failing miserably. She still had to work a whole day before he arrived. She had to be a good doctor to her patients. She mustn't think about Manolis, not at all! Until she went down to the harbour and met him off the boat at 8.30 that evening.

She showered, dressed, somehow got herself to eat a piece of yesterday's bread and drink a cup of coffee before hurrying to the hospital.

Yannis was already there, going round the patients. She'd decided he was an excellent, conscientious doctor, someone who would be a great asset to the permanent medical team. She must remember to recommend him to Manolis—and she must stop thinking about Manolis until this evening!

Patras was much happier today, having been allowed out of bed for a short while and given a pair of crutches. His wound, when she examined, it was beginning to heal and the X-rays were promising. She predicted to Yannis that they would be able to take the stitches out in a few days and put a permanent walking cast on. Well, permanent as in the next six weeks when hopefully the bone fragments would have knitted together.

"But we'll have to see what Manolis thinks," Yannis told their patient. He turned to look at Tanya. "What time does he get back today?"

"He'll be on the evening boat from Rhodes," she said calmly, though her pulses started racing every time someone reminded her of their evening reunion.

They settled their patient, answering his questions, making sure he was comfortable, before leaving his room together.

"So Manolis won't be coming in to the hospital?" Yannis asked as they walked down the corridor.

"I really couldn't say. I'm meeting the boat... well, I'll be down in the harbour anyway at 8.30 so... Was there something you wanted to see him about, Yannis?"

"Actually yes." He paused as if wondering whether to discuss it with his colleague. "I've been wondering if there would be a permanent post going in the near future. I'm enjoying my work here at the hospital and it's great to be back on Ceres again. I went to medical school in Athens and then after my wife and I married—she was a fellow student—we both worked in the hospital where we'd trained. Since she died I've felt there's nothing to keep me away from my family here on Ceres, parents, nephews and nieces, and, well, it's where I was brought up. I feel very much at home here."

She heard the crack in his voice when he spoke of his wife. She didn't want to pry and ask questions which might upset him.

"Leave it with me. I don't know what the staffing situation will be when the tourists stop coming in the winter but I'll speak to Manolis as soon as I can. From working with you while he was away I can tell we would be mad not to keep you on the team here."

She smiled at him. "You're a definite asset so I'll put in a good word for you."

He smiled back, relief showing on his handsome face. "Thanks." He hesitated. "Have you known Manolis long?"

"Since I was born—apparently. Manolis is eight years older than me. He was a friend of my brother so he remembers me from a very early age. I became aware of him much later, of course. But we…well, we didn't get together until we were both attached to the same hospital in Australia. I was still a medical student while he was a doctor, of course."

Her final sentence was delivered very quickly. "Sorry, I don't want to bore you with my life history."

"Not at all. I'm intrigued. I'm only a couple of years younger than Manolis but our paths didn't cross when I was a boy here. We lived on the other side of the island and communications weren't as good as they are today. So, when you met Manolis in Australia I presume… Look, I don't want to be impertinent but it's obvious there's a strong bond between you."

She sighed. "You could say that. We lived together for a while in Australia. We were very happy…and then it all went wrong. We've met up again six years later and…well, who knows what will happen the second time around?"

"Oh, but you've got to make it work! It's obvious the two of you are so much in love. I've never seen you together but I've heard Manolis speaking about you, unable to disguise the fact that he adores you. And every time you mention his name I just know you've got the kind of love that my wife and I shared."

His voice trailed away but then he took a deep breath and resumed in a hoarsely quiet tone of voice, "You've been given a second chance at a special relationship. You're so lucky. I'd give anything to be able to bring my wife back. Life's too short to…"

She swallowed hard as she saw the moistness in Yannis's eyes. Her heart ached to see the sadness he was fighting against.

"I won't let our happiness together disappear a second time," she told him. "I was determined even before we had this conversation but you've made me doubly determined—if that's possible!"

"Go and meet the boat tonight. Don't let Manolis worry about the hospital. I'm on duty and I'll make sure that everything's in order. I had a very responsible post in Athens. Tell Manolis I'll only contact him if it's absolutely necessary. And make sure you have a good reunion."

She reached out and squeezed his hand.

"Thank you, Yannis. And I'll make sure Manolis and I do everything we can to keep you on the hospital team."

She stood on the quayside, watching the evening ferry come in. All around the harbour lights twinkled in the waterside tavernas. The hillsides looked like dark velvet studded with diamonds. Above her the moon beamed down, lighting up the mysterious canvas of the night sky. The usually blue sea was black tinged with gold as the boat came ever nearer to her. Manolis's boat!

Would he be standing up on deck or would he be down in the saloon, chatting to friends, perhaps drinking a coffee, unaware that they were drawing into Ceres harbour? He must have done this journey so many times before that it was probably like taking the underground in London. Just another journey to get through, just another…

There he was! Standing on the deck, right at the front, his eyes scanning the quayside.

"Manolis!"

Her voice rang around the harbour, cutting through the noisy chatter, alarming or amusing the people nearest her. But she didn't care about their reaction. She was a young girl again, in love with the most wonderful, handsome, caring…

"Tanya!"

He'd seen her. He was waving madly. For a brief instant it occurred to her that they both had to maintain their decorum in hospital but out here they could behave as they wanted.

The boat was close to the harbourside now. One of the sailors threw a chain. A colleague caught it and began the arduous task of securing the large vessel as the captain cut the engines. The passengers were coming down the steps onto the boat deck. The people meeting the boat were surging forward. Now more people were calling out the names of the people they'd come to meet. She wasn't the only one excited. Manolis had disappeared somewhere in the stairwell.

Her heart turned over as she caught sight of him reaching the bottom of the stairs. She called his name again. He was smiling, waving to her now, hurrying down the landing board, making his way through the crush of people, the confusion of travellers and welcomers and…

She felt his arms wrap around her and she

turned her face up to his, her eager lips seeking reassurance that he loved her.

"I've missed you so much," she whispered against his lips as he moved to release her from his embrace.

"I've missed you too."

She felt an enormous surge of happiness running through her. She'd perhaps engineered that he would tell her if he'd missed her but she wasn't going to dwell on that.

"Is everything OK at the hospital?"

"No problems at all," she said hastily, revelling in the feel of his large hand encasing hers. "Yannis, our highly efficient and well-qualified new doctor, is on duty and he's promised to contact you if necessary. But he's given his blessing for us to enjoy our evening together and not to worry."

"Sounds good to me."

An important-looking car was easing its way through the crush of people and vehicles.

"That's our car," she told Manolis as she glimpsed the peaked-capped chauffeur driving it. "I happened to meet Alexander, our ex-mayor…"

"Our ex-patient," Manolis said with a wry

grin. "Don't tell me you persuaded him to send the mayoral car he's still allowed to use in his retirement!"

She laughed. "It was actually his suggestion— so how could I refuse?"

"Well, he's been so grateful since we operated on him and then looked after him so that he could resume his enjoyable life. That's what he said the last time he bought me a drink. I can't go into any taverna where he happens to be without him sending over a drink."

The chauffeur was opening the doors at the back of the limousine. It was so incredibly over the top for a small island like Ceres that the two of them were having difficulty in concealing their laughter as they were ushered inside into the back seat.

"Where to, sir?" the chauffeur asked.

"To Chorio. We'll get out at Giorgio's and walk the rest of the way. I don't think you could get this large car down the street where we live."

As she leaned back against the fabulously comfortable leather seat she felt his arm sliding around her shoulders.

"What a homecoming!" he whispered as his lips sought hers.

"This is why celebrities have tinted windows in the back of their stretch limousines." Tanya giggled as they both came up for air. "So they can get up to whatever they like and nobody can see them."

"I don't think we've time to get up to what I would like because we're nearly there."

"Later," she whispered. "I've prepared a special welcome-home supper in my candlelit kitchen."

"I'm not hungry," he murmured huskily, holding her face in his hands as if he couldn't believe he was actually with her again. "Not yet. But I will be…later…"

They were hardly able to contain their passionate excitement as they removed each other's clothes in the candlelit kitchen. Manolis had remembered to secure the outside door to the street when they'd come in so that they wouldn't be disturbed. He'd turned off his mobile phone. Now reassured by Tanya that the hospital was running smoothly, he could relax. He'd secretly planned to take a couple of off-duty days which were due to him and mentioned the fact that he would confirm this when he returned from London if he was sure that the hospital team could function without him during this period.

He'd actually been in contact with Yannis by phone and email while he'd been away and was impressed with the support this new member of the team was giving him. If by any chance he wanted to stay on at the end of his temporary contract, he would ensure that he was appointed to a permanent post.

All these thoughts had gone through his mind as he'd come over on the boat just now. The world didn't revolve around him. He could now relax with the most wonderful woman in his life. The woman he wanted to make his wife...if only he could be sure she would say yes. If only he dared propose without upsetting the delicate balance of their relationship.

He gathered her up into his arms, taking care not to bang his head on the low beamed ancient ceiling as he carried her up the narrow stairs to the top of the house. The bedside lights were already on. He smiled to himself. So Tanya had thought through the possibility that they might have a romantic interlude before they had supper.

He laid her gently on the bed and gazed down at her beautiful naked body. Oh, how he'd missed her!

She looked up into his eyes as she felt his tantalising fingers delicately tracing the paths she knew they both loved the most. Deep down inside she could feel the familiar awakening of her sensual desires and her body melted into the passionate embrace as they joined together in perfect harmony...

Waking up was like a wonderful dream. He was here in her bed, not miles away in another country. He looked so desirable. Even though she'd felt totally satiated by their love-making a short time ago, when he languidly opened his eyes, his lips moving in a seductive smile, his arms reaching out to draw her closer, her body melted once more with delirious passion.

The dawn was breaking over the windowsill with a rosy glow when she awoke again to find Manolis leaning over her, resting himself on one elbow.

"I didn't want to wake you," he murmured before kissing her gently, first on the lips, then nuzzling the nape of her neck before leaning back against the pillows, his arms still around her.

She'd always loved the aftermath of their love-making. The feeling that she was utterly adored by her man. This wonderful hunk who she loved to distraction. Six years ago she hadn't looked any further than the next moment of their relationship but now she was aching to look into the future. A future where she would be part of Manolis for ever, where she would bear his children, happy in the knowledge that they belonged to each other for ever and ever.

They would grow old together with the memories of a full and happy life. And, of course, the children and grandchildren.

He traced the side of her cheek with his finger. "What are you thinking about?"

She swallowed hard. "I was thinking…"

Dared she broach the subject of marriage? No, it had to come from him. She mustn't force the issue.

She sat up quickly, extricating herself from his arms. "I was thinking about making something to eat. Shall we have supper or breakfast?"

She was reaching for her robe. He leaned

across and drew her back into bed. "Don't worry about food. Come back to bed. Stay here, my princess, and I'll bring you something to drink. What would you like? Champagne? I brought a bottle from the airport and stashed it in your fridge before we came upstairs last night."

She snuggled against him, her resolve to be practical disappearing as her skin touched his.

"That's better." His arms wrapped around her so that she couldn't escape. "We ought to celebrate."

She held her breath for a moment. "What are we celebrating?"

"Our reunion, of course! I know I was only away for four days but it seemed like for ever."

"I thought you were having a great time."

"I was. Great to the extent that I could see Chrysanthe settling into the London life, getting used to sightseeing, shopping, visiting museums, and one time we even took her to the Theatre. So I was completely sure she wouldn't be homesick when I left her with Victoria."

"Well, she is her mother."

"Yes, but it wasn't always this easy when she was very small and we were trying not to row in front of her, so that she wouldn't get upset. Anyway…"

He released her from his embrace, kissing the tip of her nose before springing out of bed and wrapping a towel around his waist.

"Don't go away while I'm downstairs."

She smiled. "I wouldn't dream of it."

She snuggled down into the warm place where his body had been, watching him through veiled lashes before he disappeared down the stairs. His firm, brown, muscular legs showing beneath the towel excited her more than she needed at this moment. She simply wanted to wind down, calm her feelings and enjoy the rest of their time together this morning.

In a few minutes she found herself drifting off to sleep so she just let herself go. It had been a fabulous but exhausting night…

The sound of an explosion awakened her.

"What the…?"

"Sorry, I didn't mean to wake you. I was simply opening the champagne."

She rubbed her eyes and looked at the delightful scene in front of her. Manolis, still wrapped around by a towel, was pouring champagne at her dressing table. She could smell hot croissants.

"It took me ages to put your oven on for the croissants. I remember standing by that same oven when I was a child, waiting for your grandmother to pull out the cake and cut a piece for Costas and me. It must be positively antique by now."

He turned and handed her a glass of champagne. "To the most beautiful girl in the world."

He entwined his arm with hers as they both took their first sip together.

"Another toast!" he said, his eyes firmly on hers. "To us…to…to the future, whatever life may hold."

"To us!"

It was all becoming so impossibly formal she began to fantasise that he was leading up to a proposal. In your dreams, said the still sane voice in her head. You had your chance, girl, and you blew it.

He unwrapped the towel, threw it in the direction of a chair and climbed back into bed, carrying the tray of croissants and apricot jam. The champagne was already firmly placed on the bedside table.

She took another sip of her champagne. "How long was I asleep?"

"Long enough for me to phone the hospital and establish that we're both taking two days off duty."

She stared at him. "But who did you speak to? It's only seven o'clock."

He smiled broadly. "When I switched on my mobile I found a text from Yannis asking me to phone him this morning. He said he was going to be on duty there all night. He told me that Alexander, our beloved chairman of the hospital board and ex-mayor and very difficult ex-patient, had called in to the hospital yesterday evening to ensure that you and I were going to have two days off duty before we resumed our work."

"Whatever is the man up to?"

Manolis laughed. "I think he's matchmaking, as you would say in English. Perhaps he doesn't approve of our affair and wants us to…to make it…more formal."

She held her breath. He was leading up to it…he was…he really was. He was looking at her with a strange enigmatic expression that could only mean…

As Manolis studied her face he misinterpreted the expression of anxiety. She looked terrified! And that could only mean that she thought he was going to propose again. He hadn't given up hope but in the meantime they could continue as they were. Life was getting better by the minute.

"More champagne?" He picked up the bottle and leaned across the bed to top up her glass. A wicked thought passed through his mind that if he got her a bit tipsy she might be open to saying yes if he proposed. But would she regret it when she was sober and sensible again? Probably.

"So what's the plan if we're not going to work today, Manolis?"

"Would you like to go out to the little island where we took Chrysanthe?"

"I'd love it! We can take everything we need for a barbecue and a picnic."

"If we take some breakfast-type food, we could sleep overnight in the cabin."

He put down his glass and took her in his arms. "Would you like to sleep under the stars with the boat rocking gently on the waves as they lap the shore?"

"Sounds so…so romantic."

He began kissing her face, nuzzling her neck. She could feel his arousal as he drew her even closer.

"The boat will start rocking by itself when we

settle ourselves in the cabin," he told her with a wry smile. "But there'll be nobody there to see it but a few sheep and maybe the odd goat…"

By midmorning they were all packed up and ready to set off. Tanya had made sure that Manolis phoned London to speak to Chrysanthe because he'd told her there would be no mobile signal on the island. Chrysanthe as usual was excited to speak to Manolis and also wanted to talk to Tanya.

"We'll call you as soon as we get back home tomorrow, Chrysanthe," Tanya told the little girl.

"Tomorrow! Are you going to sleep with the sheep?"

"Well, the sheep will be on the island but we'll be sleeping in the cabin on the boat."

"Oh, I wish I was with you! Will you take me with you some time when I get back to Ceres?"

"I'll ask Daddy."

"Tanya, will you meet me at the airport in Rhodes when I come back and take me back to Ceres on the ferry?"

"I'll see what Daddy's arranged, darling. He may have planned to meet you himself."

"Oh, I meant both of you to come and meet me. My London mummy is flying with me to Rhodes and then going straight back. You could meet her. I've told her all about you being my Ceres mummy."

"I'll let you know what Daddy's planned as soon as I can. Goodbye."

"Goodbye. I love you, Tanya."

"I love you too."

Manolis was standing by the door. "What was all that about?"

"Oh, I'll explain later. Decisions, decisions…!"

"Come on, let's leave it all behind. For one day only we're going to be completely alone."

"Bliss!'

CHAPTER TEN

THE sound of the sea lapping around the boat and the movement as the gentle waves took them by turn nearer then further away from the shore created an idyllic end to a perfect day. She revelled in the warmth of her sun-tanned skin contrasting with the coolness of her pillow as she lay relaxed and refreshed by her wonderful day on the island, waiting for Manolis to come back from securing the boat to its mooring.

Everything had gone right today. They'd even seen dolphins dancing in their remote bay as if to welcome them when they'd arrived. Manolis had caught a tuna, and had been well pleased. They'd feasted royally on their barbecued fish, sheltering under the trees to escape the rays of the hot mid afternoon sun. Then they'd had a decidedly sensual, sexy siesta curled up together, a couple of lovebirds in their shady nest, before rousing each other to go for another cooling swim.

The dolphins had disappeared by this time and the sun had slowly begun to make its descent over their little island. So they'd gathered up their belongings, which had been strewn all over the small pebbly beach and begun to prepare the boat for their evening and night aboard.

Tanya had spread the sheets out in the sun as soon as they'd arrived earlier in the day and the pillows, which had been stored in a locker, had needed a good airing. But by suppertime they both agreed there was nothing more to do except enjoy the feta cheese, salad, taramosolata and spinach pies they'd bought in Ceres town on their way to the boat. Washed down with a special bottle of wine from Crete, which Manolis produced from his small wine rack in the galley, they made themselves comfortable on deck to watch the sun making its descent into the sea.

Tanya gave a sigh of contentment as it seemed to plunge into the depths on the horizon, spreading a gold and red carpet of light over the surface of the sea, which extended as far as their boat.

"Happy?" Manolis asked her.

She smiled. "What do you think?"

"I don't think I needed to ask you. I can tell that…"

He drew her against his side and together they looked out over the darkening sea before he suggested she go inside the cabin and prepare for the night while he finished up the chores on deck and in the galley.

She'd listened to him moving about above her, jumping off the boat at one point, presumably to check the moorings. And now she could hear his footsteps coming down the ladder that led to the cabin.

She smiled as he came in and began stripping off his clothes. "Everything OK? The sea's calm now. The rocking of the boat won't be a problem tonight unless…"

He moved with one virile, seductive movement to climb in beside her on the bunk. She felt his hands beginning their impossibly arousing exploration of her eager body as his lips sought hers.

"Your skin feels so cool," he whispered. "Let's make the boat rock so that you can warm up…"

* * *

They lay back against the pillows after they'd made love. She could hear a sheep bleating on the shore, probably calling to its lamb. She'd seen the mother and baby that afternoon and noted the lamb was being particularly frisky. The mother would find it soon. Yes, she heard the lamb now, calling to its mother, and then she was sure she could hear the gentle sound of the baby sucking as it fed. Or maybe she was just imagining it, she thought idly.

It was so utterly peaceful here. Not a sound except the soft murmur of the lapping water. Nothing more except Manolis breathing beside her. If only this could go on for ever, just the two of them, nothing to impede their romance, no customs and conventions to say what they should or shouldn't do.

She turned to look at him, his profile illuminated in the moonlight that was streaming through the cabin window.

"I wish we could stay like this for ever," she told him, leaning over to brush her lips across his face.

"No reason why we shouldn't." He tried to keep his tone light and mischievous, entering into the spirit of make-believe. "We could set up an annexe of the hospital here. Request that the patients be shipped out here."

She laughed. "Will you arrange that?"

"Of course! We could live like Robinson Crusoe—apart from the hospital patients, who would require some attention occasionally."

"And Chrysanthe, of course."

He smiled down at her, propped up on his elbow now. "But she'll grow up and look after us soon."

"And the hospital," Tanya said, wishing life was always as easy as this fantasy game they were playing.

She raised her head and kissed him gently on the lips. "Goodnight, darling. It's been the most perfect day."

"Another one coming up tomorrow. And then back to the real world."

"Yes." She turned on her side. "We've got a good life out here, haven't we?"

"Couldn't be better now that we've found each other again," he murmured.

She lay quite still until she felt his breathing becoming steadily deeper as he fell asleep.

It couldn't be better, she told herself. Very soon he's got to broach the subject of a permanent relationship. It's all so nebulous at the moment. He talks about the future all the time and I'm always part of it.

For the moment she'd have to be satisfied with that. Sometimes she felt she was drowning in happiness. She mustn't spoil what they'd got.

The warm sun streaming through the cabin window woke her. She stretched out her hand to touch Manolis, but he wasn't there. She could hear him moving about on deck. Throwing back the sheet, she wrapped herself in a towel and went up the tiny wooden ladder.

The morning sun had already warmed the surface of the deck. She curled up against the cushions at the front of the boat and watched Manolis pouring out a cup of coffee from the ancient, blackened coffee jug.

"I thought you might surface if I made the coffee," he said, handing her one of the small coffee cups.

He squatted down beside her. "Sleep well?"

"You know I did," she murmured in mid-sip of the strong black coffee.

He put down his cup on the side of the boat.

"When I wasn't disturbing you," he whispered, taking her face in his hands, tracing her beautiful skin with his fingers.

The coffee went cold as they made love. It was exquisite, Tanya thought as she lay back afterwards, the hot sun on her bare skin, listening to Manolis making more coffee in the galley. This life has to continue. Oh, not the make-believe Robinson Crusoe life they were emulating at the moment. A real relationship that would stand the test of time.

Her eyes were moist as she turned to watch the sheep trotting along the shoreline, its errant lamb following behind, looking docile today. Mother sheep was getting the message through that it shouldn't stay out late where there might be danger. When the sun set it should make sure it was safe with its mother.

Mother love was a wonderful thing. She found herself thinking about the baby she'd lost. Their baby. But they could have another baby…babies even! Manolis never talked about the baby they'd lost. Perhaps men didn't feel the pain of losing a baby as much as women did…or maybe they just put on a brave face and got on with life.

"Why are you looking so serious?" He was handing her a cup of fresh coffee.

"Do you ever think about the baby we lost?" she said quietly.

He swallowed hard. "Often. Especially when I'm with Chrysanthe. I think how wonderful it would be if our baby had lived. We wouldn't have split up, we would have been together all through those six years when we were both having a tough time." He looked up at the blue sky. "When Chrysanthe was a baby she helped me to forget some of the pain I'd felt at our loss. But it's always there, isn't it?"

He reached out and took her face in his hands. His voice had been so poignantly tender when he'd spoken. She hadn't realised he'd suffered their loss as much as she had.

"It must have been awful for you, just as it was for me," she whispered.

"It was…but life went on around me and I simply went with the flow for a while until the pain eased."

"I wish I could make it up to you."

"Oh, you can, you are now." He gathered her into his arms, revelling in the scent of her, which was so nostalgic of their previous affair. "Today we're going to live out our dream. No plans, no patients, no children—no worries, as we used to say out in Australia."

She laughed as he drew her to her feet so that they could both dive off the side of the boat together.

"Wow! The water's still cool." The dive had taken her breath away. As she came up for air now she found Manolis nearby, treading water.

"Cool but not cold. It's going to warm up as the day goes on." He hesitated. "I thought it would be a good idea to call in at the hospital on our way home tonight, just check that everything's OK."

"Why not? We've got to return some time."

"Meanwhile, how about scrambled eggs for breakfast?"

"Fantastic! My favourite breakfast."

He swam nearer. They trod water together while discussing the breakfast menu.

She was so glad that the macho image the Greek men liked to keep didn't exclude them from cooking when they were out in the open air. Kitchen utensils on land were regarded as OK for the fairer sex but anything to do with a barbecue or a boat was definitely their territory.

She swam back slowly and stretched out on deck, turning her face up to the sun. It was going to be another deliciously sexy, highly memorable day…

Yannis seemed surprised to see them when they turned up at the hospital that evening.

"I thought you were taking two days off duty, Manolis."

"This is only a social call. You haven't been working all the time, have you?"

"I've only just come back again. I slept all day. The team worked extremely well. I'm going to stay on till midnight and then I'll take the rest of the night off. By tomorrow my body clock will be normal again for day work." He hesitated. "There's an operation scheduled for tomorrow morning."

"What is it?"

Yannis began to explain. "It's Alexander's wife's hip replacement. He's kind of exerted pressure to jump the queue."

Manolis groaned. "I'll say he has. We prefer to send hip replacements over to Rhodes. In fact, I've put her on the list and she's got a date for next month."

"I know. I explained all that because I checked her notes and phoned him back. But he was adamant that she couldn't wait. And she also wouldn't have any other surgeon but Manolis. She remembers you as a little boy."

"Yes, yes. I'm sure she does but—"

"She's a great fan of yours—and Alexander was singing your praises over the phone to such an extent that—"

"Well, I'll have to do it! Always best to stay on the right side of the chairman of the board."

Tanya smiled indulgently. "Maybe that's why he's been so charming to us. Giving us the VIP treatment for the past two days."

"The wily old fox." Manolis frowned. "Well, I'll admit her to hospital tomorrow but I'm not operating on her till she's been fully prepared. I'll postpone surgery until the day after tomorrow. Any other problems, Yannis?"

"No, everything under control. Patras, the smashed tallus and tibia, keeps asking when he can see you."

"I'll go and see him now. No, it's OK, Tanya. You don't need to come. I'll only be a few minutes. Yannis, would you take Tanya for a decent cup of tea? I forgot the tea bags and I can see the English part of her is getting withdrawal symptoms."

The medics' staffroom was empty. Tanya put the kettle on and sat down in the comfiest chair by the window, waiting for it to boil.

"How was the honeymoon?" Yannis asked, with a wry grin.

"Wonderful!"

"And the proposal?"

She shook her head. "My English mother used to tell me an old English saying that you could lead a horse to water but you couldn't make it drink. I couldn't have made it clearer that I wanted us to stay together for ever."

The kettle was boiling. She half rose but Yannis got there first and was already pouring the boiling water over the tea leaves in the pot.

"Real tea leaves! What a treat!"

"That's how we make it in Athens."

"And here on Ceres—but not usually when we're on a boat." She sighed. "Yes, everything was perfect. So perfect that I wanted to propose to Manolis myself."

"Oh, you couldn't do that!" Yannis looked genuinely shocked. "Manolis would have been scandalised! And all his family too if the news had got out."

"But it's so old-fashioned!" She took a sip of tea to calm her frustration at the impossible situation.

"You must have realised by now that Ceres is old-fashioned. That's what makes it so charming. I always stick to the rules here. They've been bred into me and I certainly wouldn't have wanted my wife to propose to me."

"I know, I know. I was born here too, remember. I remember my English mother crying with frustration at something my stubborn Ceres-born father wouldn't allow her to do."

"Well, are you sure you want to marry a Ceres-born macho, stubborn, bossy, authoritarian—?"

"Wonderful man," she finished off for him. "Yes, I do. I'm utterly convinced about that."

"Well, you'll just have to be patient, I'm afraid. It certainly looks like it. If only I could—"

The door swung open and Manolis walked in. Tanya put down her cup and made to cross the room to pick up the teapot.

"No tea for me, thanks." He looked from one to the other again. "I could swear you two were talking about me when I came in. You both went suddenly quiet."

"I was telling Yannis about the dolphins."

"No, you weren't." He gave her a wry smile.

She took a deep breath. "I was saying how conventional you men are on Ceres. Always sticking to the old-fashioned customs where it's not the done thing for a woman to propose marriage to a man."

"There would be a scandal if that happened in my family," he said lightly, his eyes scrutinising her expression. "How about your family, Yannis?"

"The same as yours. But, then, nobody's ever tried it, as far as I know."

"Of course not." Manolis hesitated, wondering if Tanya had been asking his advice. No, she must know the conventional rules on Ceres. They'd just been having a light chat together—or had they? Could she possibly be thinking about marriage? Never had he ever thought... No, he was jumping to conclusions—wasn't he?

"Come on," he said briskly. "Let's go home and have a long soak in the bath."

"The same bath?" Yannis pretended to look shocked.

"I wouldn't like to say," Manolis replied lightly. "Otherwise I might compromise Tanya's reputation."

Manolis placed his arm around her waist possessively and began to guide her to the door.

"Whatever happens, Yannis, we'll both be on duty tomorrow."

They were both down in the kitchen early the next morning, trying to get themselves into the mood for work.

"Come on, Manolis, it's not as if we don't like our work. You'll soon be back in the saddle again."

She was leaning over him to pour a cup of coffee from the fresh jug she'd just made. He took hold of the jug, placed it on the table and pulled her onto his lap.

"I was getting used to our idyllic life out there on the island," he whispered. "I'm glad I'm a doctor but the last two days have made me wish I'd been born a fisherman like my ancestors."

"That fish you caught wouldn't have fed a large

family," she joked. "You'd have had to have a second string to your bow."

He laughed. "Quite right. OK, let's go and do some work, Doctor."

He kissed her on the lips before she could escape from his lap. They separated for their different tasks before meeting by the door to walk down to the hospital.

The pattern of their lives that evolved while Chrysanthe was in London soon became the norm. On the evening before she was due back, as Manolis lit the candles on the table in Tanya's kitchen she knew that they'd both enjoyed probably the most wonderful period of living together that they'd ever experienced.

Manolis blew out the match and looked across at her, his eyes tender and expressive.

"Are you thinking what I'm thinking, Tanya?"

"Probably. I love Chrysanthe to bits but we've had a great couple of weeks just the two of us, haven't we?"

He came round the table and drew her into his arms. "I'm looking forward to seeing my daughter again tomorrow, but this time when we've been completely alone in the evenings and that two days of fantasy on our little island without a care in the world. That was like our…"

He broke off. He'd been going to say "our honeymoon" but that would have meant he couldn't avoid bringing up the subject of marriage. And that could be enough to burst the bubble of their happiness.

She held her breath. "Like our what?"

"Like our first days together when we first moved into our flat. We were like a couple of kids."

"Well, let's face it. We were a couple of kids. I think we've both matured in the last six years, don't you?"

"Possibly," he said, a whimsical smile on his face.

He reached inside the fridge and took out the bottle of champagne he'd put in there when they'd first arrived back from the hospital.

Tanya placed the glasses on the table in front of him. They clinked their glasses together, linking arms, as had now become something of a ritual.

"I had a phone call from Victoria today."

"Yes?" She was immediately alert, waiting to hear what his ex-wife wanted.

"Apparently, Chrysanthe would like you to meet her at Rhodes airport. She wants you to meet Victoria. Don't ask me why because I haven't a clue."

"It's the afternoon plane, isn't it?"

"Yes, you'll need to be there by about three."

"Oh, so you want me to go?"

"It's by special request. I thought I'd give you the day off and you can be the perfect Ceres mummy doing the transfer from Chrysanthe's English mummy."

"I think she might want you to be there."

"Impossible from a work point of view! It's you that Chrysanthe wants to meet her. You three girls can have a pleasant chat together. Victoria only has a few minutes before she takes the same plane back to London. Don't worry, she won't bite you. She's very civilised. Now, just relax and enjoy the rest of our evening."

He came round the table and drew her into his arms. She felt a frisson of excitement at the evening ahead…

Getting off the Rhodes ferry in the early afternoon, she walked along the harbourside to the taxi rank.

It was just as well that Manolis had given her the day off today because they hadn't had much sleep. It had been as if they'd both been clinging to the fantasy life they'd led and changing to become responsible adults with a child to consider was going to somehow intrude. But they'd both agreed that the totally selfish life they'd enjoyed couldn't continue. They were both longing to have Chrysanthe back.

Tanya felt that their love for each other had grown stronger while the darling little girl had been away, but without children in their lives it would be a false sort of relationship. Sooner or later, Manolis would realise that. He had to! He had to propose sooner or later.

The taxi was drawing into the airport waiting area. She could feel her excitement mounting. It would be so good to have Chrysanthe back with them again.

CHAPTER ELEVEN

THE arrivals hall was in its usual state of turmoil. Tanya made her way through the crowds, her eyes scanning the nearest screen. Chrysanthe's plane had just landed. She moved as near as she could to the glass door where the people meeting those coming off the plane were waiting. She was lucky enough to find a seat in the corner where she could watch the door, which was now being opened.

Good sign. Hopefully she wouldn't have to wait long. She whiled away the time looking out through the glass windows, which gave a good view of the arriving coaches and taxis. A pleasant cooling stream of air was coming down from a vent just above her. Air-conditioning had been unheard of when she'd been small and had sat here with her parents, waiting to meet visiting relatives. The airport had been much smaller, much less organised and hopelessly chaotic in those days. As a child she'd wondered why on earth her parents had dragged her away from her island home to come to this noisy place to politely say hello to some unknown person. She'd had to be on her best behaviour, wear impossibly clean clothes, speak when she was spoken to and…

There she was! Her darling Chrysanthe was coming through the door, clasping the hand of a very elegant, tall slim woman whose eyes were searching around the spot where she was sitting. Her chic blonde hair was cut in a style that suited the high cheekbones and general air of elegance and sophistication.

She leapt to her feet, feeling all of a sudden hot and flustered compared to this vision who looked as if she'd spent the morning in a beauty shop but obviously couldn't have done. She must be one of these women who remained cool, calm and collected under difficult conditions.

"There she is," cried an easily recognisable little voice. "There's Tanya. Tanya, it's me, I'm home, I'm…"

And the tiny bundle of energy unleashed herself against Tanya's legs. Tanya picked her up, feeling tiny hands round her neck.

"Tanya, I've missed you so much! Has Daddy come?"

"No, he had to work at the hospital."

"Hi, I'm Victoria."

A firm, cool hand gripped hers.

"Good flight?"

"Not bad." She pulled a wry face. "I've had worse. Now, I've only got a few minutes before I've got to get along to Departures and go back to London on the same plane when they've managed to clean it out. There were so many kids on the plane it was in an awful statc by the time we got here."

Chrysanthe had wriggled free and jumped down from Tanya's arms. "Mummy, Mummy, can I go to the crèche now? I'm going to meet that girl who was on the plane."

"Yes, just a moment, Chrysanthe. I'm talking to Tanya. Now, we must have a chat. I've arranged for Chrysanthe to go into the crèche for a short time. She's been in there before and is desperate to play with her new friend."

"It's over there, Mummy! I know the way. I'll just—"

"No, I'll take you then you must stay with

the stewardess till Tanya or I come to pick you up."

"If you've only got a few minutes, Victoria, it's best if I pick up Chrysanthe."

"Good thinking! After all, you're her Ceres mummy, I hear." It was said in such a tone of approval that Tanya felt reassured that Chrysanthe's birth mother obviously didn't mind her stepping into her shoes when they were apart.

"So Chrysanthe explained that was how she describes me to her friends on Ceres."

"Oh, she talked of you all the time. I'll say goodbye now, darling. Tanya will collect you soon."

"OK. Bye, Mummy."

Chrysanthe disappeared into the crèche after a stewardess had taken details from Victoria and Tanya about who was collecting her and when.

"Well, that's a good innovation," Tanya said. "Wish they'd had that when I was a child. Hours I spent in this place, kicking my heels."

"We've just time for a cup of tea—or would you prefer coffee?" Victoria was heading over to the drinks dispenser. "It all comes out of the same container, I think, but... There you go."

They found a corner where there were two seats. "It's great to meet you at last. As I say, Chrysanthe is besotted with you. And also with the idea that you and Manolis are going to get married and give her a baby brother or sister just like the rest of her friends seem to be having."

Tanya tried a sip of her tea and put it straight into the nearest waste bin. "The tea hasn't changed!"

Victoria agreed as she also binned hers.

Tanya didn't mind the tea being awful. The bonding of the two women in Manolis's life was going much better than she'd dared to hope.

"I think it's a kind of one upmanship to have a baby brother or sister," she said carefully. "I'm not taking it too seriously."

"Oh, but you must! It's so obvious that you and Manolis were made for each other—just as it was obvious from the start that Manolis and I would never make a go of it. Talk about on the rebound! The poor man didn't know what to do with himself. He was utterly bereft. I felt so sorry for him. It was obvious he'd left his heart in Australia. He never stopped talking about you. I suppose I just wanted to comfort him at first and, well, you know how things develop when you've had too much to drink. Manolis was hell bent on drowning his sorrows. Somehow the comfort turned into sex…and then in no time at all I found I was pregnant."

Victoria fidgeted on the uncomfortable plastic chair. "Of course, Manolis did what he thought was the honourable thing and asked me to marry him. You know, they're so old-fashioned over there on that quaint little island, aren't they? I would have been content to split up at that point and bring up the child myself—well, with the help of a nanny, of course, so I didn't have to take a career break—but, oh, no. Manolis said his child had to be legitimate. His family on Ceres would… Oh, you must have come across the sort of thing I'm talking about."

"Absolutely! That's the problem at the moment with our relationship. Manolis actually proposed marriage when we were in Australia and I turned him down—for various reasons which we don't need to go into. Anyway, we have a marvellous relationship now but…well, I'm waiting and waiting for the third proposal, which just isn't coming. And I daren't propose to him because it would be so frowned on."

"Well, of course it would. Oh, it's so easy to talk to you, Tanya." Victoria broke off as she looked at her diamond-encrusted watch. "Look, we must keep in touch. I'm sure you'll find a way of prompting Manolis. Oh, there's the announcement for my departure. I'd better go. Stick to your guns because, as I say, you two were made for each other. You could stick your neck out and just tell him it's for Chrysanthe's sake. She's desperate for a baby brother or sister."

They were both laughing together now as the woman who'd been sitting next to Victoria, leaning nearer so that she could take in the bizarre conversation, got up from her seat and walked away looking thoroughly shocked.

They stood up and air-kissed each other on both cheeks. "I feel as if I've known you for ages," Tanya said, feeling relieved that their short introduction to each other had gone so amicably.

"Well, in a way you have—through Chrysanthe. I wish we had more time to chat through this problem. When you've solved it—as I know you will—please invite me to the wedding. I'll just lurk in the shadows at the back of the church and

I won't cause any problems. I won't hurl myself at the altar weeping and wailing…"

Tanya was giggling now. "I can't imagine you weeping and wailing about anything, Look, you'd better go or you'll miss your flight. I'll go and collect Chrysanthe."

She watched the slim figure disappearing through the crowds in the direction of the departure lounge. She turned as she went through the doors and waved, still smiling.

Tanya waved back. This certainly wasn't the meeting she'd dreaded. She'd made a true friend in a matter of minutes. That was a part of the relationship that would be easy. Chrysanthe having two mummies. It was the daddy who was the difficult one.

They enjoyed a smooth crossing on the ferry. So smooth that Chrysanthe fell asleep snuggled up to Tanya in the saloon. She had to be woken up a few minutes before they were due to dock.

The little girl smiled sleepily and was soon in conversational flow. A never-ending stream of thoughts and dreams had happened while she'd been asleep and she needed lots of answers from her Ceres mummy.

"Did my London mummy tell you that you and Daddy could easily get a baby brother or sister for me if you really tried?"

"I think she might have mentioned it but she was in such a hurry to catch her plane... Oh, look, we're nearly there. Daddy said he'd try to get out of the hospital in time to meet us. He's got such a busy day today."

"Mummy said all the daddy has to do is to plant a seed in the mummy. He's got this kind of injector thing. Does my daddy know how to do that?"

"I'll have to ask him. But not just now because, as I say, he will have had a busy day and he's probably tired."

Chrysanthe put her head on one side so that she could look up at Tanya and judge her mood. Grown-ups could be so weird. You could never tell what they were thinking. Best to change the subject because Tanya seemed really tense.

"Is Daddy cutting people up today? He really likes cutting up people, I think."

Tanya was relieved they'd been speaking Greek together since Chrysanthe woke up. The English tourist listening next to Chrysanthe didn't flinch at the little girl's words and smiled with complete incomprehension at the continual flow of Greek words from such a small child.

"I think he probably is. Can you pass me your jacket and I'll help you put it on."

"Is it difficult to put people back together again once you've cut them up? I mean, knowing which bit goes where?"

"Daddy's a very good surgeon so he knows exactly what to do. You have to train a long time to be able to work like Daddy does."

"I'm going to be clever like Daddy and train for a long time. I think I'd like to cut people up. It's probably like doing jigsaw puzzles. Must be fun sorting out which bit goes where. You can do it, can't you, Tanya? Daddy was telling Grandma one day that you were the best doctor he'd had helping him in the operating theatre."

Tanya took hold of Chrysanthe's hand and led her firmly towards the top of the stairs that led to the boat deck.

"Grandma said your daddy used to cut people up and he was ever so good at getting babies for people. Didn't your daddy ever tell you where he got the babies from? Didn't you ever ask him?"

"Careful on the stairs, darling. Watch your step. Hold my hand tightly for this last little bit… There he is! There's Daddy."

Manolis had somehow managed to board the ferry as soon as it arrived. He could usually find the odd grateful patient who would bend the rules and let him aboard.

"Daddy!" Chrysanthe ran forward as Manolis bent down to greet her. He lifted her high in the air and swung her round. "Daddy! You're not tired, are you?"

"Of course not. Why should I be tired?"

"Well, Tanya wants to ask you… Oh, look, there's my new friend from the plane. Let me go and see her before she gets off the boat." Chrysanthe had wriggled her way out of Manolis's arms and was halfway down his legs, scrambling to the floor.

"No, hold onto my hand, Chrysanthe," Manolis said, as he reached for the escaping child.

Tanya screamed out. "Hold onto her, Manolis. They're letting the lorries off the car deck. They're—"

A deafening thud, the screech of brakes and then an awful silence around them. The worst thing had happened. Every parent's nightmare. Their child under the wheels of a vehicle.

"Chrysanthe, darling." Tears were streaming down Tanya's cheeks as she bent to reach the motionless child beneath the wheels of the large truck.

The driver was crying as he climbed out of his cab. "I slammed on my brakes as soon as I heard you call out. I never saw her. She came from nowhere. Is she OK? She's not…?"

Manolis was on his knees, crouched over his daughter. The wheels of the truck were resting against her head. She'd received a blow to the head but the wheel hadn't passed over her.

The driver was trembling with shock. "Get an ambulance! Quick. I couldn't help it. Nobody said the passengers were on this deck."

"It's OK," Manolis said quietly to his unconscious daughter.

Tanya was at his side.

At that point the captain arrived, saying frantically, "I've called an ambulance. I'm sorry, I'm sorry! There was a new sailor in charge of disembarkation today. He shouldn't have given the signal for the trucks to start their engines and move off early like that."

He was pleading with Manolis now. "Is there anything I can do, Doctor? She's not…?"

"I just need to get my daughter to the hospital…"

"Your daughter? Oh, Manolis I wouldn't have…"

They waited in silence until the ambulance arrived and the paramedics stabilised Chrysanthe's neck and head for the journey. The normally noisy, loquacious, lovable child lay pale and motionless while they tended to her and Manolis and Tanya looked helplessly on.

As Chrysanthe was carried to the ambulance, Manolis strode through the crowd with Tanya beside him in a state of total shock. She just knew she had to get Chrysanthe to the hospital before she allowed herself to cry. She had no idea how badly injured her daughter was. She wasn't her daughter—she knew that. But that was how she now thought of her.

They all went to the hospital in the back of the ambulance, Manolis checking out his little daughter with a paramedic en route. She was very still, eyes closed but she was breathing.

As the driver pulled in to the hospital forecourt and slammed on the brakes, Tanya opened the door and got out.

A porter with a trolley arrived and, with Chrysanthe lifted safely onto it, Manolis led them all hastily straight past Reception and along to the X-ray department.

"X-ray of skull please…now!"

In a very short time Manolis and Tanya were examining the X-ray images on the screen.

"There's no fracture of the skull," he said in a relieved tone. "No discernible subdural haematoma, which sometimes happens in a concussion like this. I'll get a CT scan to make sure. If blood has collected beneath the skull it won't be a problem for me to remove the haematoma provided I can do it quickly so— Ah, Yannis, don't you agree with me that—?"

"Absolutely, Manolis. But I think you should let me take over at this point if you don't mind me saying so. You're bound to be in a state of shock because this is your daughter. I'll take Chrysanthe for a CT scan and report back to you as soon as possible."

Tanya put her hand on his arm. "Manolis, my darling, just let Yannis take over for a little while. Sit here with me for a moment. I need you by my side, my love. You're shaking with the shock of it all."

"OK. Yes, you're probably right. I think I am in shock. But, Yannis, get back to me as soon as you can."

Gently, Yannis took the motionless child from her distraught father. "Chrysanthe will be fine with me. Take it easy, Manolis, and I'll keep you informed."

The lights in Chrysanthe's hospital room had been dimmed. The child was breathing steadily but was still unconscious. Tanya clung tightly to Manolis's hand as they sat together at the side of her bed. She was exhausted but knew she would never be able to sleep even if she'd taken up the offer of the bed in the corner of the room.

"Why don't you try and get some sleep, Manolis? You've been working all day."

He tried to smile but failed miserably. "I don't expect your day has been all that easy. How did you get on with Victoria?"

"Very well. She's easy to get on with."

"Really? What did you talk about?"

"Oh, this and that. Chrysanthe mainly."

He attempted a wry grin and succeeded. "And me?"

She smiled. "Possibly."

Yannis walked in. "All the tests show there's no haematoma. She has concussion, which we all know can be unpredictable. She could come round any minute or…or we may have to wait a while longer."

"Thank God! How about the swollen arm I pointed out to you? What did the X-rays show?"

"The ulna is cracked. I'm going to take her along to the plaster room and put a cast on now."

Manolis half rose. "Do you want me to do it?"

"No, I'd like to do it," he said, firmly taking the lead.

Tanya put her hand on his arm. "Better you rest while you can. Why don't you stretch out on the bed over there?"

"I might just do that while Yannis is putting the cast on Chrysanthe."

CHAPTER TWELVE

As THE morning sun tipped over the windowsill of the small room in Ceres Hospital, Manolis opened his eyes and took in the all too familiar scene. Tanya was still sitting by Chrysanthe's bed, holding her motionless hand, looking down at her with the gaze of a concerned mother and an experienced doctor.

Twice during the last three hours he'd got up from the bed in the corner of the room reserved for the patient's relatives and tried to persuade Tanya to take some rest. But she'd been adamant that she wanted to be there when Chrysanthe came round.

She'd looked at him with those intense, beautiful eyes where the sad expression told him that she knew as well as he did that it wasn't when she came around, but if. He'd stayed with her for a short time, hoping to give her some support. But she was one tough lady who'd done exactly what she felt was the right thing to do all her life. There was no changing her.

He watched for a few moments wondering what life would be like if she ever left him. They'd split up before and it had been hell. It mustn't happen again!

He threw back the light sheet that was covering him. He was still wearing the clothes he'd worn yesterday morning. At some point he'd try to have a shower—but not yet. Like Tanya, he didn't want to leave their precious daughter. He'd seen how Tanya had completely bonded with his child. Chrysanthe was only slightly younger than their child would have been.

In fact, looking at the scene of mother and child now, he doubted if Tanya could differentiate her feelings from what she would have felt if she'd actually given birth to Chrysanthe.

Tanya looked across the room at Manolis sitting on the narrow bed in his crumpled clothes, his dark hair flopping over his forehead, and her heart went out to him. Was his anguish worse than hers because he was the biological father of this precious child? She couldn't imagine anything worse than the agony she was going through.

A nurse came in through the half-open door. Tanya looked up expectantly.

"Do you have any more results of the tests?"

The nurse shook her head. "I came to see if you'd like some breakfast, Tanya."

"No, thank you."

The nurse looked across at Manolis. "Doctor?"

"No, thank you," he said in an absent tone of voice. He stood up and walked across to the bedside. "Maybe some coffee, strong please."

He sat down on the other side of Chrysanthe's bed and took hold of her limp, seemingly lifeless hand. His eyes scanned her face for any sign of life. Then he raised her arm, which was encased in a cast. He checked on the fingers.

"They're only slightly swollen," Tanya said. "I've been working on them every few minutes."

"Let me take over now. Why don't you go and have a shower?"

She gave him a faint smile. "Do I look grubby?"

"You look wonderful, darling. But if you feel anything like I do..."

"OK, I'll go off for a short time when I've had some coffee. Find some clean clothes to put on."

The nurse brought in a large coffee pot and two

cups. Beside it she'd placed a plate with some small bread rolls.

"You must eat," she told them. "It could be a long time before…before your daughter regains consciousness. These rolls are freshly baked. I've just been out to the bakery in the harbour to get them."

The nurse hesitated by the door on her way out. She was much older than these two doctors. She'd become very fond of both of them since she'd come back to work now that her family were grown up.

"Please eat something to keep up your strength. Life must go on."

She closed the door quietly behind her.

Tanya picked up the plate and held it towards Manolis. "Sound advice. Take one of these."

Manolis dutifully finished his bread roll and took a gulp of the strong coffee.

Tanya forced something down. "This drip needs changing." She stood up. "Have we any more glucose saline in that fridge?"

"Yes, I checked a short time ago." He handed her a pack.

She scrubbed her hands and put on some sterile

gloves before changing the nearly empty pack for a full one.

"Got to keep Chrysanthe hydrated."

Manolis nodded. "I'll send another blood sample to the path lab this morning for a full blood count and checks on how her body is coping."

"She'll need to be strong when she comes round and starts…" Tanya hesitated. "Starts talking again."

Her voice cracked as she came to the end of her sentence. She looked across the bed at Manolis. "It will be so wonderful to hear that little voice chattering again, won't it?"

He swallowed hard. "Yes. It will happen, you know, Tanya."

"I know, I know." She was choking back the tears now.

He stood up and came round the bed, drawing her to her feet so that he could take her in his arms. He pressed his lips against her tousled hair, murmuring gently.

"I'm so glad you're with me, darling. I love you so much."

He lowered his head and kissed her on the lips. It was a gentle kiss, devoid of all passion but infinitely soothing to her. But what was most reassuring to Tanya was his assertion that he loved her. She couldn't remember him saying that since they'd been together in Australia.

"I love you too, darling," she whispered.

He kissed her again, before smoothing away the tears from her face with his hand.

She gave him a long slow smile as she looked up into his swarthy but still handsome face.

"I'll go and take that shower. Won't be long. Don't go away."

"As if!" He was already holding his daughter's hand, checking her pulse. "You know, as long as she's breathing and her heart is beating…"

He broke off as Tanya turned at the door, listening to him clutching at straws.

"Look, we've both been with unconscious patients who've recovered and we've been with some who haven't," she said quietly. "We're doing all we can but medical science can only do so much." She took a deep breath. "I'm hopeful."

"So am I!"

She went down to the female staff shower room. It was empty. She'd checked the contents of her locker and found a brand-new packet of cotton knickers which she'd brought over from Australia. Not at all glamorous but perfectly serviceable. She'd picked up a clean white short-sleeved coat from the doctors' clean laundry pile outside the shower room.

The hot water tumbled down, washing over her sticky skin. Yesterday afternoon, waiting outside the airport, her clothes sticking to her skin, she'd promised herself that the first thing she would do when she reached home would be to have a bath. Hours later, it felt as if she'd died and gone to heaven.

She made a point of trying not to think about Chrysanthe. Manolis was with her. A large number of the hospital medical team were devoting their combined skills and energy to ensuring that this little girl wasn't going to die.

She stepped out of the shower wrapped in a hospital issue towel, ready to face whatever the day threw at her.

Somehow, they both got through the day without losing hope. But it was a tough one. As they resumed their places beside Chrysanthe's bed Manolis reached across the bed and took hold of her hand.

"She's going to make it!" he said firmly.

"Absolutely!"

Whenever her hopes dwindled during the day she'd taken hold of Manolis's hand and they'd both said their mantra together. Heaven knew, they'd done all they could during the day. And the rest of the medical team had been amazing. They'd pooled their ideas and theories, tried every test that could possibly give them a clue as to what was happening inside that little head. There was no evidence of a blood clot.

They sat either side of the bed for a while, both of them in deep contemplation. Manolis was first to break the silence.

"An unconscious state like this could last for weeks, months, years even before…before…"

"Before it's resolved," she put in quickly as she saw him floundering to find the right words without demolishing the hope they were hanging onto.

"Exactly!" He reached across the bed with his spare hand and squeezed Tanya's.

Neither of them must admit that their hope

had grown thin during the day. Neither of them must give in to the temptation to face the medical facts of the situation. The longer this unconscious state lasted, the less likely they were to get their daughter back so that she could lead a normal life.

Tanya glanced once more at the clock across the room. Two a.m. This second night was proving harder than the first. She forced her heavy eyelids to stay open. They'd decided to take turns to have a two-hour sleep while the other watched. It was time for her to wake Manolis but he looked so peaceful. She'd give him another five minutes.

Her heart missed a beat as she thought she saw the faint fluttering of Chrysanthe's eyelashes. She leaned closer, not sure if it had really happened. Chrysanthe was completely still again. The small hand remained cold and motionless in her own. She'd imagined it.

Tomorrow she was going to play some of Chrysanthe's favourite CDs to see if there was any response to the music. She remembered a young patient in Australia who'd been roused from a coma after several weeks by the sound of his favourite music. But unfortunately his brain had been damaged by the length of his vegetative state.

That wasn't going to happen to Chrysanthe. Oh, no! She was going to…

That was a definite fluttering of the eyelids! She hadn't imagined it this time.

"Manolis, Manolis!"

He was immediately awake, throwing back the sheet, padding across the floor in his bare feet.

"She's opening her eyes. She's opening…"

A strange gurgling sound came from Chrysanthe's mouth as her lips began to move. They leaned over her, clinging to her hands.

"Chrysanthe," Manolis said gently. "Can you hear me, darling? Can you…?"

The eyelashes fluttered again and she opened her eyes. For a few seconds it appeared as if she couldn't focus her eyes on the faces hovering above her. And then she uttered another sound, a gentle animal sound like a small lamb calling for is mother.

"Mmm…mmm…Mummy. Mummy." Slowly she turned her head towards Tanya, then Manolis. "And Daddy…"

"Oh, thank God! She's OK." Tanya choked on her words as she leaned down to kiss the child's forehead.

"I was dreaming," Chrysanthe said slowly and very faintly. So faintly they both had to bend down as closely as they could to catch what she was saying. "I was dreaming. We were on the boat…. The sun was hot…"

She closed her eyes and became quiet again as if the effort of those first few words had exhausted her.

"We must be patient, not rush her progress," Tanya whispered.

Manolis nodded, his heart too full of emotion for him to speak.

Several hours later, Tanya had made her small patient comfortably propped up against her pillows. The few words she'd spoken had indicated that all her faculties were well and truly in place. Time, the great healer, would do the rest.

For the next seven days they all lived in the small hospital room. The medical team involved with Chrysanthe's care had insisted that they keep their patient in hospital until they all agreed that she was back to normal again.

Manolis and Tanya both agreed. They knew the odds on a case like this and didn't want to take any risks until Chrysanthe was out of danger. But exactly one week and two days since she'd been admitted to hospital the entire team agreed that the patient could go home.

It had helped that both parents were doctors and would pick up on any sign of deterioration in the patient's condition. Even so, Alexander had insisted that they have round-the-clock nursing care on hand at home. He didn't want the parents to tire themselves. And he'd also insisted his chauffeur drive them home. Only the best for the sleeping princess.

It was Alexander who'd first called her that when he'd visited her the first day she'd woken from her sleep as he'd put it.

"You were like Sleeping Beauty," he'd told her.

"Was I really?" Chrysanthe's eyes had become wider than they'd been since she'd fallen into her coma. "Am I a princess?"

"I think you are," Alexander said. "And so do your mummy and daddy."

And Manolis had whispered into Tanya's ear, "There's nothing wrong with our daughter's brain!"

"She'll soon be running rings around us again," Tanya said happily.

It seemed as if the whole of Ceres had heard about the doctor's sick child who'd woken from her coma. People were lining the streets down by the harbour. As the mayoral limousine drove slowly along the water's edge they were actually cheering.

"I'm not really a princess, am I, Daddy?"

"You are to us, my darling. And for the people of Ceres you're a princess for the day."

"Wow!"

Manolis closed the bedroom door behind him and walked quickly across to the bed.

"Don't you think we should leave the door ajar?" Tanya said, as she snuggled back against the pillows to admire Manolis's athletic muscles as he stripped off his robe.

"No reason why we should," he said firmly. "There's a trained night nurse in Chrysanthe's room ready to come and alert us to any change in her condition. But the way our little princess has been behaving today—even with the inconvenience of the cast on her arm—leads me to believe that she's completely OK."

He climbed into bed and drew her towards him.

"Completely OK? Is that your clinical diagnosis now, Doctor?"

"It is indeed. It's you who needs your head examined."

"Me? What clinical signs have drawn you to that ridiculous conclusion?"

"I've done a lot of thinking while we were going through the awful crisis of almost losing our precious child. I can't live without you, Tanya. Everybody who knows us—friends, colleagues, the world at large—acknowledges we are a great couple. Made for each other is the phrase often bandied about."

"Yes," she said, drawing out the word as slowly as she could.

"Chrysanthe regards you as her mummy now and—"

"Manolis, I think I know where this is going—"

"Please, hear me out before you start saying anything. I know what you're going to say but—"

"You do?" She was impatient with hope that he might, he just might be going to…

"Tanya. Six years ago I asked you to marry me and you turned me down—twice! But I'm going to ask you again anyway because it doesn't make sense to go on as we are doing. I agree with the general consensus of opinion that—"

"Ask me, Manolis," she said, breathlessly.

"What?"

"Ask me to marry you."

"Well, against all the odds I am going to ask you to marry me even if—"

"And I'm going to say yes."

"But no matter what you think or… What did you just say?"

"I'm thinking that if you were to get out of bed and go down on your bended knee I could give you my answer—the answer I've longed to give you for ages. So please put me out of my misery. The suspense is killing me."

He looked completely stunned as he climbed out of bed and went down on one knee. He felt as if he'd turned into a robot. He was simply obeying orders. This couldn't be the girl who'd turned him down twice admitting that maybe, just maybe it could be third time lucky.

He swallowed hard. "Tanya, will you marry me?"

"Of course I will. What took you so long?"

Waking up in Manolis's arms, the details of the previous evening when Manolis had proposed to her were sketchy to say the least. But the love-making that had ensued had been out of this world. That bit she did remember! She remembered him climbing back into bed after his proposal, covering her with kisses as she settled into his arms.

And waking up in his arms just now, stretching out as a new day began. A day when she would have to start planning the wedding of the year! Everybody on the island would want to be invited. And her mother and stepfather and all of Manolis's enormous family.

He was opening his eyes, drawing her closer to him.

"Manolis, darling, before we…before we… I need to talk to you about the wedding so… Mmm…well, perhaps later…"

* * *

Just over a month from Manolis proposing to her they were standing in the beautiful church on the hill overlooking the entrance to the harbour. Neither of them had seen any point in waiting to tie the long-awaited knot.

Tanya was intrigued by the knots of ribbon that were being made around the two of them by the priest and his assistants in front of the altar. It was at this point that she began to realise that she was actually going to be Manolis's wife after all these years of longing.

She felt little fingers touching the ivory silk of her fabulous long gown and bent to see Chrysanthe admiring the texture and feel of the hastily but beautifully made garment. Two of the best seam-stresses on Ceres had worked flat out to have it finished in time for the wedding of the year.

She bent down to whisper to Chrysanthe, who was chief bridesmaid, looking pretty and demure in her ivory silk mid-calf-length dress. She'd wanted a long dress like Mummy Tanya but Manolis was so afraid she'd fall over in her exu-berance at some point during the long day that he'd suggested she would look better in a shorter version. He'd X-rayed her arm yesterday and decided that after six weeks in a cast the ulna had healed perfectly. She'd parted happily with the cumbersome plaster regretting only the fact that she could no longer show off all the signatures from friends and family.

"Are you OK, Chrysanthe?" Tanya whispered.

Chrysanthe nodded. "Why are they tying you up with Daddy?"

"To show that I'll always be with him."

"And me?"

"Of course."

Chrysanthe squeezed Tanya's leg encased in the layers of silk. "How much longer do we have to stay here? I need to go to the loo. I ever so need a…"

Tanya could see Victoria watching from the back of the church. She nodded her head down towards their daughter. Victoria hurried forward and put out her hand to take hold of the chief bridesmaid. Tanya smiled and mouthed her thanks as mother and daughter walked off down the aisle.

This was the first contact she'd had with Victoria that day. She'd arrived at the last minute and had been keeping a low profile at the back of the church. Not exactly lurking, as she'd so poignantly put it when they'd talked about the possibility of a wedding, more trying to remain unobtrusive in her chic silver grey designer suit and impossibly high stilettos.

The service continued all around her with the priests chanting loudly and the guests becoming restless in the hot airless church. They'd deliberately chosen the wedding to be at the end of the holiday season so that the island wasn't too crowded and the weather was still good.

The weather today was hot, almost too hot, but she was so happy that she hardly noticed. Only the sight of the ladies in the congregation fanning themselves with their wedding programmes made her hope that the service wouldn't last much longer.

As soon as it ended, she and Manolis were surrounded by their guests before they'd had chance to leave the altar.

"Let's go outside," Manolis suggested to the nearest and dearest of his family, who were clinging to him, congratulating him, kissing him and generally holding him back from his bride, who was signalling to him they should leave.

They finally found a way of getting together

before walking down the aisle and escaping into the fresh air, hands firmly clasped together, Chrysanthe holding onto Tanya's skirt so that she didn't fall over in the crush of people all trying to reach her Mummy and Daddy.

"Thanks, Victoria," Tanya said as she passed by the London mummy.

Victoria smiled. "Glad I could help. You look absolutely gorgeous. And so do you, my poppet." She bent to kiss her daughter. "What a good girl you've been."

Chrysanthe beamed and looked up at her Ceres mummy. "Are you and Daddy married yet?"

"We are," Tanya said as they posed for the cameras outside the porch.

"When will you start to make the new baby?"

"Let's talk about it later, Chrysanthe. Smile now for the camera."

She looked around at the enormous crowd. It had been a mammoth task to get all her relatives here. She had a particularly special smile for her brother Costas who'd miraculously phoned a couple of weeks before to say that he was going home to Australia from South Africa to introduce his new fiancée to his mother.

According to their mother—who was now coming forward to join the large family photograph to be taken on the grass to the side of the church under a large tree that would give them some shade—it hadn't occurred to Costas that the family might be worried about his whereabouts. So he'd simply got on with his work out there in the back of beyond.

Tanya's mother came closer to her now, kissing her cheek before moving to the appropriate place for the mother of the bride.

"I think Costas's fiancée is going to be a good influence on him," her mother whispered, before taking up her place.

Tanya smiled. "About time someone took my brother in hand."

"I heard that," Costas said, coming up to stand behind her. "Hey, Manolis. We've got a lot of catching up to do, my friend. How about I meet you tonight for a drink—after this show, of course."

"Sorry, Costas," Manolis said. "I've got an important date with the most wonderful woman in the world."

Costas looked around him. "So when's she arriving?"

"Quiet, Costas!" Tanya's mother said.

"And now just the bride and groom by themselves!" the fraught photographer boomed above the laughter and chattering.

Manolis took hold of her hand as the crowds moved back. "Happy?" he whispered.

"What do you think?"

"A kiss! The wedding kiss," the photographer called.

"This is the best bit," Manolis said as he drew her into his arms and kissed her. His kiss deepened and the crowd cheered.

Tanya pulled herself gently away. "Later," she whispered.

"Promise?"

Her eyes shone with the promise of the night to come, their first as a real married couple. "Can't wait…'

EPILOGUE

CHRYSANTHE climbed into bed, snuggling down between her mummy and daddy, taking care not to speak until they opened their eyes. Since her baby brother had arrived they'd been keen that she shouldn't talk and wake him up when they'd just got him to sleep. She glanced at the cradle at her mummy's side of the bed. He was a very small baby. She hoped he would start growing soon. He hadn't seemed to get any bigger since he was born three weeks ago.

Tanya lay very still, pretending she was still asleep. Baby Jack had needed two breastfeeds in the night and it seemed only a short time since she'd fed him.

Chrysanthe stared hard at her mummy. She was sure she wasn't really asleep. Perhaps if she just whispered to her, that would be OK.

"Are you awake, Mummy?"

"I am now."

"It's morning time. Look, the sun's shining outside. Daddy, can you see the sun?"

"Mmm?"

"The sun. It's shining. Must be time we all got up, don't you think?"

"Morning, darling." Manolis planted a kiss on his daughter's cheek before reaching across to his wife and kissing her on the lips. "How were the feeds last night? I think I might have slept through them."

"I think you did. But I forgive you because you had a long busy day at the hospital yesterday whereas—"

"Mummy and I did nothing all day yesterday but look after Jack. I loved it! Do I have to go to school today? I know it's Monday but—"

"Don't you want to go to school and tell all your friends how brilliant it is now that you've got a baby brother?" Tanya said.

"Yes, OK. But will you come and meet me and bring Jack in the pram?"

"Of course I will. Now, don't make a noise as you climb out of bed. Just go back to your own room for a couple of minutes and start putting on your clothes."

"OK. You'll come and help me, Mummy, won't you?"

"Yes, I'll be with you in two minutes. I just want to discuss something with Daddy."

Chrysanthe paused at her mummy's side of the bed and looked gravely at the eyes that were firmly closed again.

"You know, I told you it was easy making a baby, Mummy. You did really well. It seems to be the looking after the baby that tires you. But you've got me to help you, haven't you?"

Tanya opened her eyes and smiled at the child who now seemed as if she was her true firstborn. "Of course I've got you to help me. I don't know what I'd do without you, darling."

She held out her arms and closed them around Chrysanthe. "Now, off you go and start getting ready for school, my love."

"What was it you wanted to discuss?" came a sleepy voice as the door closed behind their daughter.

Manolis drew her into his arms and she snuggled as close as she could get.

"I've forgotten. It will have to wait until this evening."

"Like everything else," he told her in his most seductive, provocative tone. "Unless…"

"Not now, Manolis!" She moved out of range and put her feet on the floor. "You won't be late tonight, will you? Because… I've forgotten what I was going to say again! It must be all these broken nights."

"They won't go on for ever. Can't wait to have you all to myself again." Manolis looked down at his sleeping son. "But I wouldn't be without this wonderful gift you gave me, darling. As Chrysanthe just said, you did well making our baby."

She laughed. "It was an absolute pleasure, I assure you."

"We could maybe make another one in the not too distant future," Manolis said gently.

She blew him a kiss. "It would be fun trying…"